Jane Seaford has had a number of careers: mother, academic, IT consultant, bakery manager. She currently focuses on her writing. Her short stories have been placed highly commended or short-listed in international competitions. Many have appeared in anthologies or magazines. Several have been broadcast. She has also worked as a freelance journalist. Her first novel, *Archie's Daughter*, was published as an e-book in 2012, and another novel *The Insides of Banana Skins* is due out in 2016. Jane is joint fiction editor for *takahē*, a New Zealand literary magazine. Her website is janeseaford.com.

Also by Jane Seaford

Archie's Daughter

Praise for Archie's Daughter

'Once I began reading "Archie's Daughter" I couldn't put it down, or rather couldn't close my laptop.' Rocky Hudson

'Archie's Daughter really is an admirable piece of work; I'd definitely want to read Seaford's next novel.' Ije Kanu. Editor, LiteraryFiction.bellaonline.com

'Excellent narrative of daily life, including the blight of depression, that holds the attention till the end.' Doc Lyn Saunders, Amazon UK review

'This is one read that you won't want to miss.' http://www.mentalhealthy.co.uk

Dead is Dead

and Other Stories

Jane Seaford

The characters in the stories in this collection are fictional. Any resemblance to a real person, alive or dead is coincidental.

This collection first published in 2016

ISBNs

    978-0-473-37121-0 (softcover)

    978-0-473-37122-7 (Mobi)

    978-0-473-37324-5 (epub)

    978-0-473-37325-2 (pdf)

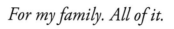

For my family. All of it.

Thanks to Belinda O'Keefe for her excellent proofreading, to Karen Baker for her wonderful cover, to Janet Wainscott for giving wise and considered advice on the publishing process, to Juliana Feaver for her support and assistance on many aspects of producing this book, to Shirley Eng for endless discussions on writing over the years and to the other members of my various writing critique groups: Hikatea Bull, Felicity Cutten, Joan Eddy, Janice Healey, Pat Land, Mary Fitzgerald. Wendy Williamson and Karen Zelas.

Contents

Dead is Dead

The two hens lay draining by the path that led from the kitchen to the house. They lay with their throats cut, the blood slowly oozing, their feathers rusty-red and limp. Jennie, the little girl, watched the slow oily movement of the blood and held Tim's hand.

'Are they dead?' he asked. Silly Tim, only three.

'Course they are. John killed them.'

'Will they get alive again?'

Jennie sighed. 'Dead is dead. When you're dead you don't get alive again.'

Boobah came round the corner and laughed at them. He bent and peered at the hens.

'Not ready yet,' he said. Later he and John would pluck them and pull out their insides. Jennie had watched them doing it before. And then John would cook them and Allan would bring them into the dining room, covered in sauce and her parents would eat them and so would their guests. Boobah stretched and walked along the path to the kitchen. Jennie watched the soles of his bare feet as he moved. She loved their paleness, the way they were lighter than the rest of his dark skin. Jennie loved Boobah. When Daddy called him in the evenings, he'd pad into the living room, his bare feet making no noise, and Daddy would ask him to pour the whisky and he'd say 'Yes Massa.' Jennie, sitting by her mother in her nightie, would watch as he handled the bottles and glasses, putting in ice, squirting soda from the siphon, bringing the tray round to Mummy and Daddy and guests, too, if there were any. Boobah would be silent, he wouldn't laugh or smile and Jennie would look up at his smooth proud face, his dark eyes, empty now, and wonder why he had to pour the whisky when it was her parents who drank it.

Sometimes her father would shout at Boobah and the other servants in Hausa and they wouldn't say anything. They'd stand and bend their heads and leave slowly and quietly when the shouting finished. Boobah was the small boy but he was the tallest and darkest.

'Why are you the small boy when you're so tall?' Jennie would ask him and he'd laugh. He was often laughing when Jennie was with him. Boobah was the small boy, John was the cook and Allan was the steward. Once John and Allan had had other names but when they became Christians, they'd changed them. Mummy had told them that. And Daddy had said with a snort, 'Christians when it's Christmas or Easter and Muslims for Muslim holidays.'

Allan came out of the house, and called to Boobah in Hausa. They set off for the compound and Jennie and Tim followed them, down the path and round the corner behind the fence. The three wives were singing together as they pounded grain in tall wooden pots with long wooden poles. Two of the women had babies tied to their backs. The older children looked up as Jennie and Tim stood at the edge of the compound. Jennie would have liked to play with them but Mummy said they shouldn't. Once she'd come here when the families had been eating. They'd all sat – women, men and children – round a large pan of dark thickly-sauced stew, taking a white paste in their fingers, dipping it into the stew, using it to absorb gravy and secure pieces of meat, before transferring it to their mouths. How Jennie had wanted to join in, to sit cross-legged round the big pan, use her fingers, mould the paste, dip it in stew, taste the meat, lick the gravy from her lips. But she had her meals at the dining table, using knives and forks and spoons and served by Boobah and Allan.

'Let's go back,' said Tim and tugged at her hand. Jennie followed him back to the garden where the garden boy was cutting the grass with a scythe making a crackly slicing noise with each stroke. He was only young and didn't live in the compound. And he didn't talk to the children, never answered when they asked him questions, just went on cutting. Mummy said it was because he didn't speak much English.

Jennie lay next to her sleeping mother on her parents' bed. She was staring at the sun through half-closed eyes. The sun seemed to be popping out of itself over and over again in disks of different colours, red, orange, yellow, almost white.

3

Jennie felt nearly asleep; she wondered if the sun was really popping coloured disks or if it was her eyes doing tricks. She squeezed her eyelids a bit closer together and the disks started to pop faster, then she widened her eyes and the popping slowed. She lay still, moving nothing but her eyelids, mesmerised by the sun's activities.

Daddy burst into the room.

'Grace, Grace. Have you seen my gun?' His voice was urgent and accusing and the sun stopped popping. Jennie moved her eyes into different shapes but the sun just sat blandly in the sky. Mummy, woken abruptly, was speaking in a slurry voice. 'What? What is it, Eric?'

'My gun, I can't find my gun.' Mummy sat up. She was wearing only underwear. Jennie squeezed her eyes once more, but the coloured disks had gone. She rubbed her face with the backs of her hands in disappointment. Daddy was standing by the bed shaking his clenched hands.

'Grace, have you put it somewhere?'

Mummy stood up, took her dress from the chair beside the bed and as she pulled it over her head said, 'No, of course not. I have nothing to do with it. Have you asked Allan, or one of the others?' She pulled the skirt of her dress down over her hips and started to do up the front buttons.

Daddy turned and a long cross sound came out of his mouth. He turned back again and poked his head forward. 'I can't find Allan and the others deny all knowledge of its whereabouts. I'm supposed to be going shooting tomorrow.' Mummy had finished her buttoning and went to sit at her dressing table. She stared into the mirror before picking up a lipstick and making her mouth red. Once Jennie had knelt on that stool, looking into that mirror, putting on her mother's creams and make-up. She'd nearly finished, dipping her finger into a final sticky pot when she'd felt a sharp pain on her bottom. She'd looked up, shocked. Her father had been standing there with an angry face and upraised hand.

'How dare you use your mother's stuff!' he'd yelled and Jennie had opened her mouth and howled. Not from pain, that had been momentary, but from unfairness. She'd only been doing what her mother did every day and she'd been smacked for it.

'Grace! Are you sure you haven't seen it?' Daddy was pacing the room.

Mummy turned to watch him.

'No, no I haven't. We'd better look for it. We'll get all the servants and have a thorough search.'

Tim was poking the ants with a stick. He and Jennie were squatting down, watching as the insects moved into disarray and then, after scurrying around frantically, regrouped into the long thick marching column that came through their garden, went up and over the house, past the compound and out into the bush beyond.

'Be careful, they sting,' said Jennie, poised to jump and run should one of the ants come too close. Tim gave the column an even harder poke and the ants scrambled. Jennie jumped up, pulling Tim.

5

'Jennie, Tim. Come here at once.' Mummy was standing on the veranda. 'Quickly.'

'No,' said Tim. 'We're playing.'

Mummy was coming towards them. She picked Tim up and took Jennie's hand. Tim squirmed. 'Don't want to be picked up.'

'Do as you're told, Timothy,' Mummy said and Jennie looked up at her. Her face was white and her mouth was a hard red line. Jennie moved closer to Mummy; leant against her legs and took a bunch of her skirt in her hand.

'Come on,' Mummy said and, pushing Jennie, she hurried into the house, put Tim down and shut the veranda doors.

'We're going to stay somewhere else for the night,' Mummy said when the door was shut. 'Come up and help me with the packing.' Mummy's voice was watery.

'Why?' said Tim.

'Yes, why?' Jennie asked. Mummy looked at them both. She seemed to be thinking.

'Because Daddy's gun is missing and so is Allan. There's nothing really to worry about but Daddy and the police think we should go somewhere else.'

Jennie started to shiver.

'Want a biscuit,' said Tim and started to suck his thumb. Mummy shook her head.

They heard the sound of the car arriving and stopping, the slam of the car door and Daddy's voice calling. 'Grace, you ready? We must be going.'

Daddy took the suitcase and the box of food. As they left

the house and he locked the door with a key, Jennie heard the buzzing of flies and saw the dead hens still lying like a bruise by the path.

Suddenly it was dark and Jennie, sitting next to Tim in the back of the car, felt him lean against her as he slept. Then Daddy was lifting her out of the car and carrying her into a room lit by a kerosene lamp.

Jennie could hear voices outside. She opened her eyes and sat up, blinking. It was morning and she could see Tim in a bed next to her and across the room her parents sleeping.

'Mummy,' she called and stood up. 'Mummy,' she called more urgently and went to the front door; it was locked.

'Jennie,' Mummy whispered and Jennie turned and went to her.

The knock at the front door made Jennie tremble. Daddy left the breakfast table.

'Yes. Who is it?' he asked.

'The police guard. We have news.'

Daddy turned the key in the lock and went outside closing the door behind him. Jennie looked up at her silent mother; the light in the room was pale, menacing. She put down her cereal spoon. The thought of food sliding down her throat into her tummy made her feel ill.

'Eat up, Jennie,' Mummy ordered. She shook her head.

'Go on,' said Mummy, lifting the cereal spoon and putting it into her hand. Jennie took a mouthful, with a great effort she swallowed. She shuddered and forced another spoonful into her mouth.

'Eric,' Mummy said, her voice coming from miles away. 'What is it?'

Daddy came and sat down. He put his elbows on the table and leant his face into his hands. Jennie swallowed her mouthful and put down her spoon. Daddy spoke, his voice dry and thin. 'They've found the gun. They've found Allan. He's committed suicide.'

'Oh Eric.' The way Mummy spoke made Jennie want to cry.

'What's mitted suet side mean?'

'Oh Timmy, love. Eric, the children.' Mummy put her hand on Tim's head.

'What does it mean?' Tim persisted.

'Shut up Tim,' Jennie said, scared of the explanation. She watched Mummy and Daddy looking at each other; watched as Mummy licked her lips and shook her head.

Then Daddy spoke. 'It's when somebody kills themselves. Allan has shot himself with my gun.' Jennie wondered if she was going to be sick.

'Is Allan dead?' Tim asked and Jennie stood up and walked round and round the room, trying to stop the feeling in her tummy from getting worse.

When they went home, Daddy had to tell Allan's wife. Jennie watched as he went to see her and soon after she heard the wail coming from the compound, high-pitched, hopeless, heart-breaking. It went on through all the hot afternoon.

'Is Allan's wife still very sad?' Jennie asked Boobah some days afterwards. Boobah looked at her and his eyes were no longer smiling for her. 'I don't know. She and the children had to leave, their room was needed for the new steward and his family.'

My Beautiful Dad

It is not easy being the son of a man who wants to become a woman. The day before my father told us that he and my mother were parting, I heard him answer his phone and after the first 'Hello' his voice rose. It sounded high, but gravelly, too, and he massaged his throat with the fingers of one hand. He laughed in a funny way and tossed his head as if he had long hair. I went into the garden and ran three times round the house trying to stop my tummy feeling tight and empty at the same time. Something frightening was happening but I didn't know what.

Late that evening Julia came into my bedroom. She sat on the end of my bed and whispered, 'Do you want to know a secret?' She is my sister, two years younger than me. The weekend before there had been a party for her tenth birthday. Soon after the last guests had left, I found my mother crying in the kitchen but she pretended not to be when she saw me coming in. She turned away to scrape leftover food from the dirty plates into the rubbish bin. I leaned on the table with both hands and watched her. There was a fly, one of those horrid big ones, by the window, buzzing and buzzing as it tried to get through the glass. I didn't say anything, nor did my mother. She just went on dealing with the plates and the fly went on buzzing. I watched the fly becoming more and more frustrated and out of the corner of my eye I watched my mother as she worked. Once she'd finished scraping the plates, she loaded them into the dishwasher. She is very beautiful: tall with long blonde hair.

After a while my father came in. Silently, he stood next to me and, like me, leaned on the table with his hands. My mother stopped loading the dishwasher and turned to face us. The noise of the buzzing fly filled the kitchen as my parents said nothing.

Now, days later, here was Julia in my room and I felt as if the whole house was about to explode. I sat up, blinked and leaned against the bed head.

'Well?' Julia said.

'No,' I said, scared. I did not want to know the secret; sure it was something horrible about our family.

'You do,' she said. I shook my head. It was dark, long after the sun had set, but still we could see each other, shadowy figures in the dimness of my room. Julia moved up the bed and sat close to me. She leant forwards and said, 'Dad puts on a wig that makes him look like Mum.'

I put my hands over my ears. Julia pulled them away. She put her face almost next to mine and said, 'I saw him. After supper.' She sounded fierce. I didn't know if she was telling me in the hope that I could explain it to her or because she thought it would upset me. Which it did. I didn't know why he would want to wear a blonde wig. But I knew it was part of whatever it was that had, increasingly over the last few months, been making us all unhappy. And scared.

Next day our father didn't go to work. He didn't come down to breakfast, either. It was the last week of the summer holidays and so Julia and I, and our mother who is a teacher, weren't at school. As we were finishing our toast, Mum said she was going out for the day. She spoke in a tight voice as if she didn't want to be saying what she did.

'Who'll look after us?' Julia asked.

'Dad,' Mum said and she was gone.

Julia put the last of her toast into her mouth and crunched it, screwing up her eyes. She was almost crouching, her back bent and she wouldn't stop looking at me as if daring me to say or do something that she could react to. I knew that she wanted to make a loud noise, a shout or a scream, that she could say was my fault. I tried to ignore her. I looked away and stared out of the window. Sounds came from upstairs; a mild sort of bumping. Later I realised that it was Dad pulling his suitcases out of the cupboard where they were stored. He came down soon after and looked at the kitchen table: the dirty plates, a slice of cold toast in the rack, blobs of marmalade that Julia had spilled, butter softening in its dish.

'Right,' he said as if we'd all agreed to something. Julia got up and went to him. She put her arms around his waist and clung on. He massaged her shoulders, absently; hardly aware of what he was doing. 'We'd better clear up this mess,' he said. 'After that I've work to do in the garden. I want to make it tidy for your mother… I love her very much. Never forget that,' he added. I thought it was a strange thing to say. And even later, in the afternoon, when he'd told us he was leaving, I still didn't understand it.

After we'd cleared away the breakfast things, we worked in the garden. We mowed the lawn, trimmed the edges, weeded the flowerbeds and vegetable plot. Then he took us in the car to the garden centre where he bought two big wooden tubs, a big bag of potting compost and a mass of herb plants. He told us what the names were but I can't remember them all except that one of them was called rosemary, which I thought was strange as it was the name of the prettiest girl in my class at school. On the way home Julia asked if we could stop for ice cream and Dad said no, he was taking us out for lunch and we could have some for dessert. All this was making me feel as if we were preparing for something bad to happen, like a huge storm or an invasion by an enemy force.

Dad put the tubs on the terrace just outside the kitchen. Then he fetched the big spade and the little trowel from the garden shed. I had to use the spade to fill the tubs with compost and he dug holes with the trowel, put the herbs in them and patted them down. Then Julia watered them. He stood and watched, leaning on the spade. I think he was nearly crying. Somehow I knew then that he was to leave that day.

'Your mother always wanted pots of herbs near the kitchen. Now she has them,' he said.

He took us to the restaurant where he and Mum always went for their wedding anniversary dinner. I think Julia would have preferred hamburger and chips. Before the food came, Dad's mobile rang and he jumped up and turned away from us before he answered. I heard his voice go high again and watched as he bent his arm back to touch the bald patch on the top of his head. When he sat down again he didn't say anything for a while.

We sat on the terrace when we got back while he told us that although he and Mum loved us very, very much, it was impossible for them to go on living together even to keep us as a family, and so he was going to move somewhere else. All the time he was speaking, I stared and stared at the two tubs of herbs until I felt dizzy and they didn't seem real any more. Julia kept asking why he had to go. 'Why? Why? Why?' she asked. She didn't want an answer; she just wanted to fill the place up with noise.

Dad stood up, very slowly, and said he needed to finish packing. I went upstairs with him, lay on the big double bed and watched him as he folded his clothes and put them in the suitcases. He took a big black bag and went into the spare room. When I tried to follow him, he said he needed to be on his own. I waited on the landing and helped him carry his stuff downstairs. I wanted to see what he'd put in the black bag but he had wound a strap round it and fastened it with a little padlock that I couldn't open.

That evening long after he'd gone, when dark had come and I was asleep, I woke up and heard my mother crying. I crept slowly across the landing and climbed into her bed. I lay quiet and still, thinking that maybe she didn't know I was there. But after a bit, she stopped crying and she turned over so that she was facing me.

'He didn't want to go, you know,' she said. 'I made him… he…' She let out a soft, sad moan.

Julia and I saw him every other weekend. Nearly a year after he'd left, he told us that he had a new girlfriend. A few weeks later, we met her and she looked just like Mum. Tall, beautiful, long blonde hair.

'Ha,' Mum said when Julia described her. 'Narcissus. That's what he wants to look like. He wants to be a sexy blonde. Remind him when you see him that he needs to explain what's going on. No, I'll tell him. Now.' She went to the phone, dialled and, not quite shouting, her voice clipped, she said, 'They have to know. The truth. Who you are. Rosalie. Not Derek. Rosalie.' She banged the receiver down and started to cry. I went upstairs to my room and sat on my bed, shaking, knowing that something even worse than Dad leaving was happening.

The next time he collected us for a visit, we drove for quite a long way on roads we didn't normally use. I had got into the back of his car when he'd arrived as that felt safer. Julia sat next to him and chatted. He hardly responded. He parked the car under a tree and took the picnic bag and a rug out of the boot. We climbed a gate, walked in single file down a path and came to a riverbank. He laid the rug on the ground, knelt down and started unpacking the food. He did all this without speaking and even Julia stopped talking. We could hear the sound of the river moving fast along its bed, the occasional cry of a bird and in the distance the throaty noise of a tractor working. Dad unwrapped egg sandwiches and sausage rolls; he poured lemonade into beakers. He sat back on his heels.

'I have something to say that you'll find hard to understand,' he said. I waited for more but the words didn't come for a long time. I looked down at my sandwich. I had only taken one bite and was still chewing it. The bread and the egg were dust in my mouth. I swallowed and almost choked. I raised my beaker and drank; the lemonade was too sweet. I sat and waited while Julia continued to eat. She reached for a sausage roll and when she'd finished it, took another. Dad stared into the distance.

'Are you having another baby?' Julia asked, her mouth still full of food.

Dad turned to look at her. He blinked as if surprised to see that she and I were still there. 'No,' he said. Then he started the story. Beginning when he was a little boy. He had loved to dress in his sister's clothes. Even his mother's when she wasn't around. He liked the way they smelled, their texture and the feel of them next to his skin.

'I knew I was a girl, really,' he said and stopped for a bit.

'But you were a boy. You must have been. Girls become women and boys become men,' Julia said. She was frowning, not understanding, a little frightened. I was shivering; I was terrified. I was sure that I was about to lose my father. I was thirteen and couldn't imagine being anything other than a boy. Girls were enticing, soft-skinned and different. I fantasised about touching them but not about being them.

'Dad!' Julia almost shouted.

'Sorry,' he said and continued his story. He liked girls, he said. He had many, many girlfriends. Some of them let him wear their clothes. He and a woman he nearly married used to go out together in the evenings, he in a wig and her clothes. They pretended to be twins.

'Then I met your mother. The most lovely woman… I wanted to be… I wanted to marry her. But… she hated that I liked to dress like her. When, finally, I said I wanted to truly become a woman, she asked me to leave.'

'If you like to dress as a woman, are you gay?' Julia asked. I had been thinking that, too, but it didn't quite fit with what Dad was saying. 'We've been learning about gay stuff in sex ed,' Julia added when at first Dad did not reply.

'Have you?' Dad seemed interested in what Julia had said. 'As a woman I am gay,' he told us.

'You're not a woman,' Julia insisted.

'But I am,' Dad said and I wanted to run away, far up the riverbank and into the mountains where the water came from.

'You've got a willy,' Julia said. 'I've seen it.' I stood up and moved away. I found I could not run. I walked to the nearest tree and leant against it. My face was hot but I was still shivering. He came over to me.

'I am so sorry,' he said. 'So very sorry. But I love you both. You and your sister. Even when I become a woman, I will still be your…'

'Father?' I squeaked.

'Parent,' he corrected.

Dad continued to be our father. When he came to see us it was as a man although he was becoming rounder and softer-skinned because of the hormones and other treatments. One Saturday in the summer before I went to university, he said that his girlfriend had left him because he'd decided to take the ultimate step and have the operation. He was sad, Julia was angry, I didn't know what to feel. That evening I phoned him to say that I would like to meet him as a woman.

I push open the door to the café and there is... Rosalie; quite beautiful, long blonde hair, long slender legs elegantly crossed. She wears earrings that hang almost to her shoulders, silver bangles on each smooth arm, a short skirt, high-heeled shoes, a lacy blouse buttoned up to her cleavage, the hint of breasts. She holds her hand there, the long fingers fiddling with the top button, wanting to undo it. I gasp; it is not easy being the son of a man who is becoming a woman.

Matilda, the Determined Woman

Standing on the pavement, Matilda had screamed and screamed. She thought it would make her feel better. It didn't. A bus drove past when she was in full throttle, mouth wide open, throat exposed, and heads had turned to look at her. She watched the necks swivelling as the bus moved along and was tempted to stop screaming and stick out her tongue instead. It didn't seem appropriate for a middle-aged woman and, more importantly, was too much effort. Now here she was, limp and uncertain, a rag doll with no will of her own. She looked down at her dangling hands and decided to go home and start again. Or had she decided? She stamped her foot and saw a man in a suit raise his eyebrows as he passed her. I have not chosen this, she wanted to say to him. I am considering a philosophical issue: whether I have freely chosen my actions or if they have been caused by factors outside of my control. And so, I am not mad I am merely exploring, trying to find out if I am in charge of my life or not. You too, she wanted to say, are stuck. Like me, you do not know why you are who you are.

'Or maybe we do know; I opting for eccentricity and you for convention,' she said aloud, gesturing with both hands to emphasise the point. The man had disappeared around a corner, but the words reached two women coming from the opposite direction. One frowned at Matilda who turned and walked quickly back to her little house, making an effort not to mutter to herself as she went.

She stood by the kitchen window, gazing out at the building site next door. There were four workmen wearing hard hats, as well as a digger, a great deal of mud, several piles of rubble and a heap of sadness. One man was talking, pointing something out to the others, including the driver of the digger, who took off his hat and scratched his head. He put it back on and climbed down to join his colleagues. They were arguing, Matilda surmised.

They are trying to hide the sadness by burying it, she thought. They are pretending it isn't there; that there aren't unsettled memories and disrupted past lives all about. She opened the window and yelled out, 'Jack and Freda didn't want to leave. They were forced to. Now Jack's dead.' The workmen ignored her. Or perhaps they couldn't hear her. Matilda closed the window. Jack had fallen ill a few weeks after his children had insisted that the couple move into an old people's home. She must get on, she told herself. What had and was happening next door was beyond her control.

'I am determined to get through my tasks,' she said. And laughed. 'I am determined,' she repeated, taking sheets from the hall cupboard and carrying them into the spare room. After she'd made the bed, she fetched a duster, beeswax polish and the vacuum cleaner. When everything was clean and smelling delightful, she went into the garden, picked a small bouquet of flowers, which she put in a vase, standing it on the spare room chest of drawers.

'I hope you appreciate all I am doing for you, Mum,' she said. She looked at her watch. In an hour it would be time to fetch her from the airport.

'Fifty! I can't believe that my little girl has grown so,' Mum had said on the phone a few weeks ago. 'I'll come for your birthday.' Matilda gritted her teeth. What, she wanted to say, if I have other plans? What if I want to spend the day getting drunk, the evening dancing in clubs with my friends?

'You can take time off work. A week, I'll come for a week.'

'Yes,' Matilda said, sighing, but softly. 'I've started a course. Part-time. Philosophy. If it goes well I might carry on and get a degree,' she told her mother and held her breath.

'Why do you want to do that? At your age. Haven't you better things to do?'

Matilda shook her head, said nothing, let the words seep in and hurt her, creating bitterness at the back of her throat. When Ted had left her, some months previously, her mother had insinuated that it was her fault.

'A nice man, I always thought. Needed to be properly looked after, not taken for granted.' And, 'A wife should be welcoming when her husband comes home at the end of the day.' These were the things that her mother said. And more.

Matilda shut the spare room door. Yesterday she had

shopped on the way home from the office. In the evening she had cooked. Now that everything was ready, she would work for a short time on her course assignment, the one that had sent her out to scream on the street. Or had it? Had she chosen to do that or had her reaction been determined by causes she could barely understand? She sat at her desk and read the title of the essay she had to hand in on the day her mother was due to leave, '*Do we Humans Choose Our Actions, or is Everything we do Determined and Free Will an Illusion?*'

'I don't know. I don't know if I care,' Matilda shouted. Maybe for once Mum was right and she shouldn't have started this course. It was unsettling her. No, that wasn't true, she has never been settled, but life now seemed to be becoming increasingly out of control. She sat back, thinking of the last time she'd been in the house next door. It had been the evening before it was to be demolished and the day after Jack died. She had gone in, the back door was unlocked, and stood for a few minutes in each room, remembering the old couple who had been living here when she moved in next door. She imagined those who had come before. A hundred years ago this pretty little house had been one of the first on the street. From countryside a suburb had developed. It made Matilda dizzy to think about it and about all the things that might have taken place on this land, all the people who had known it in some form or another. She didn't want the little house to be replaced. She liked it just the way it was. Probably there had been those who had felt like that about the land before it had been built on. The idea troubled her. The destruction of a home she'd known well disturbed her.

Next day when she'd returned from work the house had mostly gone. Only a few bits remained, sad, abandoned, crying out to be rescued. It was the evening she'd started her current assignment. She read the suggested texts, went to bed confused and dreamt that when she spoke no one could hear her.

Now, Matilda sat staring at the essay question, aware of time passing, writing nothing. Twice she went to the kitchen window to look out at the workmen and the digger moving mess about. Eventually it was time to leave. She would take a bus to the airport and bring Mum back in a taxi.

'Oh, no dear, far too much,' Mum said after Matilda had served the evening meal. She poked at the lasagne with her fork, ate a little, taking sips of wine between each mouthful. 'Red would have been nice,' she said as Matilda suggested a second glass. Finally her mother said it was her bedtime, 'Not that I sleep well,' she offered as she headed for the door.

'I'll warm you some milk and then I need to work on my course assignment,' Matilda said.

'No working, you're on holiday.'

'Yes. But I have a deadline. I have to write an essay.' Matilda told her mother the title.

'Stuff and nonsense,' was the response. 'Why bother?'

'I'd rather be creating a delicate love story but I can't explain delicacy, I know nothing of love and as for creating, I'm not brave enough to think that I can,' Matilda explained. She wasn't sure where the idea had come from; she felt that she had neither chosen to think nor to express it. Her mother snorted and left the room.

Next morning there were some happy birthday emails for Matilda. Her mother came into the room as she was reading them and sat at the table, saying nothing, the room filling with unspoken complaints.

'I'll give you your presents after breakfast,' Mum said. There were two: a pot of night cream for older skin and a self-help book for single women.

'Thanks,' Matilda said, resisting the impulse to cry.

She told her mother she'd arranged to meet a few friends for a drink – 'They're looking forward to meeting you,' she lied – and that afterwards she'd booked a table for just the two of them at a nearby restaurant.

'Oh no, darling,' Mum said.

'No what?'

'No, I don't want to have drinks with strangers. And as for eating out… rich food and my digestion. You know.' She sighed. 'You go, though. I don't want to spoil your evening.'

They went for a walk once Matilda had phoned to tell her friends she couldn't meet that evening and to cancel the restaurant booking. They passed the next-door site, stopping to peer in. Matilda thought about what was happening there and how affected she was by the change from old house to three modern units. She thought, they'll sit as if they've always been there, as buildings tend to do, as if they had the right to be there and all that has happened in the place before doesn't matter. She opened her mouth to tell her mother how she felt but closed it again.

After lunch her mother rested and Matilda sat watching the men through the kitchen window. At first they worked slowly, the digger removing soil, the hole for the foundations growing deeper. There was a shout. One of the workmen raised his hand signalling the digger to stop. Matilda opened the window and looked out. All four of them were in the hole, bent over. She could see their hard hats in a huddle and hear their voices. The digger driver ran back to his machine, climbed on and switched it off. Matilda opened the kitchen door, went out onto the deck and leant over the fence.

'What's happening?' she called. One of the men looked up and shook his head. Then they all climbed out of the hole. The one in charge was talking on the phone.

'Bones,' Matilda heard him say as he came close to the fence. She shivered. The men stood about, as if not knowing what to do: one was examining his hands; another was moving his arms back and forth as if he were marching. Almost as soon as the man in charge ended his call, his phone rang.

'What are you looking at?'

Matilda turned to see her mother in the doorway. 'The workmen. They've found something on the site. I think.'

'A cup of tea would be nice,' Mum said.

'Right,' Matilda said. She went back to the fence and called, 'Is there a problem?'

'Yes,' said the man who had been examining his hands. He came to the fence. 'We've found a pile of… the remains of a skeleton, maybe more than one. Buried. Old, human most likely.' He sounded excited. 'Got to stop work. Police are coming to examine them. Bad job,' he concluded.

'Tea,' Mum ordered.

Later, when they went shopping to buy food for Matilda's birthday dinner she let her mother decide what she wanted to eat. In the end after examining almost every item in the meat counter and telling Matilda that she should choose, Mum opted for lamb chops, frozen peas, potatoes; lettuce, cucumber and tomato for a salad. Not much of a celebratory meal, Matilda considered, looking at the items in her trolley. The chops, red in their plastic packet, made her think of the pile of bones that had been found where Freda and Jack had once lived. Maybe the building would have to stop because the site was an old sacred burial place. She liked that idea. She hoped it was true.

'I suppose you want some fizzy wine. None for me, I can't take it,' Mum said. Instead, Matilda picked up two bottles of red and, at her mother's insistence, an expensive chocolate cake.

'I'll pay for that,' Mum said, though she raised her eyebrows when the woman at the till told her how much it cost.

Matilda woke the next morning to the sound of the digger next door. She jumped out of bed, pulled a jumper on over her pyjamas and ran out onto the deck.

'Hey,' she called. 'Hey.' One of the workmen strolled over. 'Why are you back? What about... the bodies you found?' she asked.

He laughed. 'Dogs. Not human at all. No issue. So we carry on.'

Matilda went back into the house without replying and burst into tears.

When her mother came into the kitchen the slow shuffling sound of her old slippers seemed so sad that Matilda gave a high-pitched sob. Her mother patted her on the shoulder and asked, her voice gentle, what the matter was. Matilda could not say. She did not know. There was so much disturbing her. Ted leaving, Jack's death, the site next door where a home had been destroyed, her struggle with her essay, above all her sorrow that she couldn't have a loving relationship with her mother. Was she how she was because of the way her mother had raised her? And if she was then her mother, too, was the product of her upbringing. If you believed this then how could your life mean anything? You were merely a cipher, nothing in yourself, just a tiny fragment of an inevitable history.

'I am just an ant. We are all ants,' Matilda said.

Her mother sighed and sat down. 'I don't understand you,' she said.

Matilda thought of dinner last night when she had held her breath, refused to respond to her mother's comments: on the food – 'Mint sauce would have been nice' – on Matilda's marital state – 'Shame Ted can't be here for your birthday. I'd have done my best to keep a good man like him' – on her university course – 'What good's all that thinking going to do you? Truth is truth whatever philosophers say about it.' At last when her mother had taken her hot milk into her bedroom Matilda had opened her mouth for a silent scream, leaning on the kitchen bench. Feeling drained, she closed her mouth. Screaming, silent or otherwise, was no solution, she realised.

'They've started work again next door,' Matilda said now as she stood to make tea and toast for their breakfast. 'There were no human remains.'

'That's a relief,' her mother said.

'I feel the opposite,' Matilda said. 'I wanted the work to stop.'

'So you were hoping there'd been a murder next door. The victim buried in the grounds.' Mum grunted disapprovingly.

'No, I thought maybe... the remains were old... that the place was somehow special.'

'You're such a daydreamer. And you think the world's a much better place than it is. Always have. In spite of evidence to the contrary, the warnings I've given you over the years and the way things are turning out for you.' Mum reached for tea and took a satisfied sip.

Matilda breathed in as rage took hold of her and then let her go. She wished she could tell her mother how she felt about everything that was troubling her, about how she wished the two of them could be close, about the effort she made into doing what she thought was right. About how difficult it was for her to stuff any part of her life, and the world about her, into categories. How upsetting it was to consider that she had no free will. How she might even be programmed into feeling like this.

'Mum,' she said, making a decision, attempting to control one aspect of her life. 'A week is too long for us to be together. I'm going to change your plane ticket. I'll pay for you to leave today. It's for the best.'

'My, my,' her mother said. Matilda noted that her reaction was one of anger not of sadness.

That afternoon, Matilda, feeling as if every single muscle in her body was clenched – the ones that controlled her face being held the tightest – saw the taxi arrive, turned from the window and cleared her throat.

'Mum. It's here. Time to go. And... I'm not coming to the airport with you.'

Her mother, sitting on the sofa, glared at her. But she stood up and put on her coat. Matilda fetched the suitcase, walked to the front door, opened it and stood waiting as her mother made slow progress towards her.

'Well,' Mum said once she was outside. The driver came over to carry the luggage.

'Bye, Mum,' Matilda said. There was no reply. Matilda watched as the taxi drove off. She felt dreadful.

She went to her desk and, under the essay title, wrote down all that had happened over the last few days ending with her decision to tell her mother to leave early. Her last sentences read, '*Asserting myself has not brought happiness, rather the opposite. But then, did I choose to send my mother away early or was it something I was compelled – determined – to do?*' She would probably fail the assignment, she told herself, giving them a true story instead of reasoned argument, but at least she'd shown how seriously she had considered the question. She wished she'd been able to find an answer.

One of Those Days

When Mum came in from the bedroom, she had pink cream on her face but you could still see the other colours underneath, especially just below one eyebrow where there was a rim of black coming through. Her lips looked sore, too, swollen and bitten and when she yawned, it was almost as if she was trying not to cry. She walked through to the kitchen end of the living room.

Tansy started moaning, looking up from the floor where we were sitting cross-legged with all our dolls around us, 'I'm hungry, we've had no…' she began but I pinched her to shut her up. It wasn't the right time to whine. It wouldn't do any good asking to be fed. It was one of those days.

'Trixie hurt me!' she yelped and Mum looked up from filling the jug.

'Cut it out, you two,' she said. 'I've got a headache.'

Tansy turned her mouth down and made it tremble. But I grabbed her arm, hurting her to stop her being silly and I leant over and whispered in her ear, 'Shut up, shut up, shut up. You'll wake Pete if you don't give over.' She pouted but

I could see from the way she raised her chin and put her face on one side that she was beginning to understand.

Although Mum was staring out through the drizzle into the back yard as she waited for the water to boil, her eyes had their dull, blank look, as if they didn't want to see. She had her arms crossed and was smoking.

'Shit,' she said suddenly, 'what are those bloody boys doing out there in pyjamas?' She lit another cigarette from the old one, which she dropped into the sink. It made a fizzing sound in the dirty water. Mum started to cough. Tansy was watching her as she hugged her best doll, the only one still with all its legs and arms, close to her chest. Her mouth was working as it does when she's not sure.

Mum took a big puff and breathed out a thick stream of smoke. She pushed the window open. Cold air came in and Mum leant out. 'You, Kevin, Grant, come in here right now,' she yelled and started to cough again. 'More effing work, more effing work for me,' she complained as she made tea. 'Soaking wet pyjamas to wash and dry. And in this weather.' I could hear our brothers still playing outside.

Mum pushed the window further open. 'Get inside, now,' Mum called more loudly and I shuddered. She'd wake Pete; she'd wake the baby. She banged the window shut and went to the door. As the boys came in, she hit them, first one then the other on the backs of their heads.

'Now,' she said, 'get yourselves dressed and stay inside.' She looked down at the muddy marks on the floor. 'Trixie,' she called to me. 'Make yourself useful for once and clean this mess up.' She spooned milk powder and sugar into two mugs of tea and taking them with her went through the hall and into the bedroom. Sometimes I hate being the eldest.

After I mopped up the floor I looked again in the fridge, as if it somehow might have filled itself since I had last opened it earlier, trying to find breakfast for us all.

'I am hungry,' Tansy said. I shrugged. That morning, we'd shared the last of the stale bread, spreading it with a thin layer of jam and now there was nothing left to eat.

'Let's look for money,' Kevin said, coming out of the back room where we all slept. He had dressed in dirty jeans and a jumper that was much too big. The big bruise on the side of his head was turning yellow. Sometimes the grown-ups drop coins in odd places and if you're lucky you can find enough to buy something from the corner dairy. Kevin, Grant and I looked everywhere, feeling between the cushions and reaching under the sofa and chairs, while Tansy sucked her thumb, still cradling her doll.

The baby started to make little squeaking noises, almost but not quite crying. Just lately he'd stopped the loud screaming he used to do, as if he'd learnt that it doesn't do any good. I went into the hall and rocked the pram. Kevin counted the few cents we'd found: not even enough for a small chocolate bar. Grant rummaged in one of the ashtrays and pulled out some longish cigarette butts. The boys put them in their mouths and pretended to smoke. They gathered up the empty beer tins, shaking them to see if there was anything left them in, drinking the dregs when there was, making faces at the vomity taste.

Just as the baby stopped whimpering there was a loud

knock at the front door. 'Nana,' Grant said, putting his butt back in the ashtray. But Nana didn't push into the hall as she normally did and when I opened the door, there was June with Brad. Her mouth was creased and floppy under the thick greasy lipstick she was wearing. It had made a bright red mark on the tip of her cigarette and her hair had gone blonde.

'S'pose Pete's still in bed,' June said and I nodded. 'Too bad,' she said, 'he's having his eldest son for the rest of the weekend.' She pushed Brad through the door and I watched as she walked up the path and away in her high heels that looked silly below her fat white calves. She teetered slightly on the wet shiny pavement. She'd been Pete's girlfriend before he came to live with Mum, even though she was nearly the same age as our Nana. I shut the door and looked at Brad and he looked up at me. He was almost four, the same age as Tansy, but he could hardly talk and he still wore nappies. Drool was dripping down his chin and he was holding tightly onto an empty box with both hands. I pushed him into the living room and started to rock the pram again.

The baby wouldn't shut up. The whinging sound went on and on and then he gave a sharp loud yelp, and then another and another. The bedroom door banged open and there was Pete, standing and yawning. He was wearing underpants and a T-shirt and smelled sour.

'Shut the eff up,' he shouted and when I'd breathed in, I was scared to let the breath out again. He was staring at me; his eyes were red and there was a vein throbbing in his neck.

After he'd hit me (it didn't hurt too much, just a light bang on the side of my neck), I ran into the living room. Tansy, Kevin and Grant were huddled together by the window.

Brad stood alone, squashing his empty box. 'D d d,' he said when he saw Pete who asked, 'What's he doing here?' and gave a big sigh as if he was doing his best and the rest of us were holding him back. He clumped through to the kitchen area and opened the fridge door. 'Who's drunk all the Sprite?' he yelled and stood leaning on the bench, rubbing his face. Our Nana keeps asking Mum what she's doing with a man so young, but Pete's a real grown-up. He had his twenty-first birthday the day after the baby was born and disappeared for quite a long time; nearly a week. Mum cried when he came back. She said it was because she was so glad to see him, she thought he'd gone forever.

When I said, 'I wish he hadn't come back,' a little bit too loudly, Mum pulled me to her. 'What did you say?' she asked. She put her face close to mine and I could see spittle between her lips. I don't like it when Mum becomes mean and I shook my head and tried not to tremble.

'You're hurting,' I said. Mum's fingers were pinching my arm where she was holding me. She dug her nails in so that I almost cried out.

'You're lucky to have Pete here,' she said with the witch voice she sometimes used. 'He's a darn sight better than your real useless father.'

When she let me go, she pushed me away and I stumbled and fell against the table, banging my elbow, which hurt my funny bone and I couldn't help crying.

Now Brad started to cry. He sometimes opens his mouth for no reason that I can see and this loud noise comes out. The baby was whining again and the rain stopped being drizzle and started falling heavily. When it does that, it sounds as if someone's dropping pebbles on our roof, over and over.

'Chris' sake,' Pete shouted. He came through the living room, cuffing Brad as he went. He lifted the baby from the pram and shook him till the whining stopped.

Then he shook him some more, saying, 'That's right, you be quiet or you'll get some real punishment.' He grunted as he almost threw the baby back into the pram. Then he pulled the sheet and blankets up so that only the top of the head was showing and went back into the bedroom, banging the door. By now Brad had stopped crying and we could hear Mum and Pete talking, the voices going up and down. We all listened and when suddenly it was silent, we all looked at each other, waiting to see what would happen.

We heard Mum giggle. Tansy smiled at me and the boys stood up. They picked up their cigarette butts and swaggered round the room, pretending to be big men. Brad laughed and I noticed that the rain had stopped.

This time when there was a knock at the door, it was Nana.

'Well,' she said, coming in and looking round. 'I suppose the two of them are still in bed?'

She picked up Tansy, who wrapped her legs round Nana's middle and held onto her tightly. Brad tottered over and stood clasping both her legs. Although she was our Nana and not his, Brad seemed to prefer her to other adults.

'What have you got for us?' Grant asked, looking at Nana's big brown bag. She comes to see us almost every Saturday and she always brings treats to eat.

'Let's clean the place up first,' Nana said, putting Tansy down and we all helped, even Brad, clearing up the mess the grown-ups had made the night before and tidying away our toys. The sun had started to shine and Nana opened the windows, letting out the stale, crowded smell. She had brought a big bottle of milk, a tin of Milo and two sorts of biscuits. She made us drinks and we sat round the table, like a real happy family, eating until there was not a crumb left, while Nana had her mug of tea and smoked a cigarette.

'Time they got up, your mum and that Pete,' Nana said, after she'd washed up and I'd helped to dry. 'And the baby must be due a feed.' She knocked on the bedroom door. 'It's me,' she called, 'there's tea made. I'll take the kids to the park. You two better stir yourselves. It'll soon be evening.'

I helped Tansy dress her best doll and then we all went out. All except for the baby, who was lying quiet in his pram.

It was beginning to get dark when we came home, still licking the ice creams Nana had bought us. Mum was sitting in the living room and Pete was out.

'He's gone to the shops,' Mum explained, lifting Tansy to sit on her knee. She smiled up at us all. She'd put more cream on her face, smoothing it over the places she wanted to hide. Everything seemed almost normal.

Nana said she must go soon, but she sat for a while, leaning back in the chair, looking tired. Pete came home. He gave Nana and Mum a beer each, took one for himself and put the rest in the fridge. I looked in the supermarket bag. There was a packet of cheese, a loaf of bread, lots of different flavoured chips. My tummy rumbled.

'Did you get nappies for Brad?' Mum asked. He was beginning to smell.

'Forgot,' Pete said and he grunted.

'We need them,' Mum said.

'Effing kid,' Pete shouted. He drained his beer, took another one from the fridge and left the house, banging the front door as he went.

'Well,' Nana said.

'Don't you start,' Mum said.

'I'll just have a look at the baby and then I'll go,' Nana said. She heaved herself up from her chair and went to the pram in the hall. I watched as she gently untucked the blanket a little, bent to touch the baby's face. I saw her frown, reach into the pram, pull back all the bedclothes and lift the baby out. She looked at him, sighed, shook her head, rocked him, pinched his cheek.

She came quickly into the living room and went to Mum, holding the baby tight. 'This child's injured,' I heard her say. 'I'm taking him straight to hospital.'

'No,' Mum said, reaching out her arms.

'He's cold, he's barely breathing,' Nana said.

'There's nothing wrong with him,' Mum said, standing up.

Nana looked at her, holding the baby against her breasts with both arms. She peered into Mum's face. 'He's been hitting you again. And the little one. I'm taking this child, now, and I'm calling the police.'

As she was going out of the front door, we heard Pete's car coming back.

'What you doing with my son?' he asked as he climbed out, still with his beer can in one hand. Nana ignored him and went running to her car. I wondered how she was going to drive with the baby in her arms. We were all in the hall by now, watching. Nana had managed to open her car, get in, close and lock the door. Pete was banging on the car roof. I don't know how she did it, but Nana's car lights went on and she drove away. Pete chased her, yelling, but then she turned the corner and was gone.

He came back inside. He was breathing hard. 'What the hell was that all about? She's kidnapped the baby.'

'She said he was injured,' Mum said. She was shivering; Tansy was clinging onto her leg with one arm, cuddling her doll with the other.

'There's nothing wrong with him,' Pete was almost roaring.

'She says she's going to call the police,' Mum said. Her teeth were chattering now.

'Interfering old bitch,' Pete said. He'd raised his hand. I didn't know which of us he wanted to hit. Kevin, Grant and I slunk back into the living room.

'D d d,' Brad said, looking up at Pete. Pete kicked him and he started to cry.

'I'm leaving,' Pete said. 'I've had enough of this place, had enough of that old busybody.'

'Stay, please.' Mum started to cry. She picked up Tansy and came into the living room. She sat on the sofa pulling Tansy onto her knee. Tansy dropped her doll, closed her eyes, started to suck her thumb and leaned back on Mum who was reaching into her pocket for her cigarettes. I saw her hands were shaking, so I went to help her, finding the matches and striking one for her. She leant forward to take the flame and her hands as they touched mine were cold.

Pete went to the fridge and we watched as he took out all the cans of beer, piling them into the plastic bag alongside the bread and cheese and chips. I wondered if I dared to ask him not to take the food but then I realised I was no longer hungry.

'Should have gone ages ago. I'm fed up with all these kids and the way they do exactly as they like. No discipline in this house,' Pete said as he took the loaded bag and walked through the living room and out into the hall.

'Don't leave me,' Mum called, but he'd gone, the door slammed one more time.

Brad, who'd been standing by Mum, bent to pick up Tansy's dropped doll. He knelt down and, holding its legs, started to bang it on the floor, over and over. Mum just sat smoking; her eyes like glass in spite of the tears that still dripped down her face. Most of the pink face cream was gone, so that her bruises and the black eye showed. I wondered who she was crying for. Probably Pete, I decided as the thin plastic head on the doll cracked open and Brad crowed in triumph.

Runners

The beam of the headlights tunnelled into the darkness and a rabbit ran in front of the car, its tail scutting white behind it. Phoebe braked, drove slowly, imagining the pounding of the big hind legs, the beating of the frightened heart.

'Whas that?' asked Merlin from the back, leaning forwards. 'A rabbit,' he answered himself. 'Get it, Phoebe. We'll have it for tea tomorrow.'

'No,' said Phoebe. Merlin sank down into his seat, the rabbit veered off the road and her mother, sitting next to her with Aquaria on her knee, gave a gentle snore.

Half an hour later Phoebe drove onto the grass behind the bach. She turned off the engine and sat in the blue-black darkness, listening to the swish and whoosh of the waves crawling up the beach and then pulling slowly back. Everyone was asleep; even her four brothers sprawled together in the back of the car. Phoebe sniffed, taking in the crayony smell of boy and the salt and fish scent of sea and sand. This was the first time they'd been here without Dad, the first time she'd driven the three hours from town, the first time she'd crammed her family into the old car; her full licence was only a week old. Time to wake them, to unlock the creaking door of the bach and hope that the memories inside didn't spill out and start Mother crying again.

The next day Phoebe felt as if she could run forever. She loved the feel of damp sand on her bare feet, the clear light of early morning tipping the crests of the waves, the endless stretch of yellow beach, the emptiness. The cool, sea-fresh air filled her lungs and she imagined it as a kind of pure fuel that would keep her going all day. Nonetheless she stopped, panting a little. She bent and took a deep breath. Then, feeling an uneasy happiness, she knelt down and stared across the ocean at the far horizon. All this space, and just her in it. Here she was not the eldest child, the daughter of the hippies, the one who ran the family after the father left.

After a while, she put back her head and opened her mouth wide, letting out a deep wail that went on and on.

When it was finished, she lay on the sand in a starfish shape, exhausted. She hadn't meant to make that noise, hadn't known she wanted to. She sat up and stared back at the bach, the tree behind it and the parked car. Inside were her family and soon they would be waking and wanting her, knowing what needed to be done to prepare breakfast but somehow unable to do it without her there.

As she came back into the bach, Merlin was telling the others what to do.

'Arthur, fill the kettle. Noah, look for the matches. Titus, stop playing with the cereal…'

None of them was taking any notice, except for little Aquaria. 'What shall I do, Merlin?'

'Wash that dirty face,' said Phoebe, closing the door. 'Mother, why don't you get dressed? I'll sort this mess out.'

'Shall I…?' asked Mother, shaking her head slightly. She was sitting on the easy chair wearing one slipper and thin pyjamas with holes in and missing buttons. Her hair was tangled and she looked as if all night she'd been dreaming sad dreams.

'I'd have left you, too, if I'd been Dad,' Phoebe said under her breath. But she sighed gently and forced a smile, feeling Mother's sorrow pull at her own heart.

'I'm trying, Phoebe,' Merlin said in his hoarse fifteen-year-old voice. 'They don't do what I say.' He slumped onto the kitchen chair with the broken back and looked down at his bare feet, bending one big toe upwards as if it could, somehow, offer comfort. Phoebe put her hand on his shoulder. Of all of her brothers, he was the one suffering the most from Dad's absence.

'You lot, get your togs on and into the sea. I'll have breakfast ready for when you're back. Merlin is in charge so do what he tells you. And make sure you all look after Aquaria.' Life would be easier, Phoebe thought, if they had proper names: Pat, Anne, Mark, Nick; those would have done. And there'd be less teasing at school. Maybe even Dad leaving would have caused less comment. And another thing, there was so many of them. Six, and there would have been a seventh. Phoebe thought of the poor stillborn baby that had come too early, just a few weeks after Dad had run away. Not that he'd been much use when he was there, getting stoned and drunk. Having a good time was what life was all about, he said. He despised money, he said, but was happy to take it when it came his way. Property was theft, he said, but he encouraged Mother to sign the papers when Gran gave her this family bach after Granddad died.

Phoebe banged the wooden spoon onto the table. In spite of it all, she missed him. He made them laugh, he played great games, told stories that never ended, let them know how wonderful he thought they all were. Most of all he'd made Mother happy.

Later, they played cricket on the beach.

'You can bat first,' Noah said, offering Mother the prized position. But she frowned and shook her head. Her eyes were glazed as if she wasn't sure where she was nor why she was there.

'Mother will watch,' Phoebe said, spreading a rug firmly on the sand. She put a pebble on each corner to hold it down in case the wind came up.

'But,' said Noah, not understanding.

'That was kind of you,' Phoebe told him.

For a few days after it had happened Mother had said nothing. She pretended that Dad was still living with them, that he'd just gone out for a little while. But Phoebe had known he wasn't coming back. That first evening when Mother spoke, she had sounded as if glass was breaking in her throat, although the words she used were cheerful.

Earlier, Phoebe had found the note, screwed up on the kitchen floor. After she read it, she'd gone outside and had stood leaning against the wall by the back door breathing in great sobbing gulps of air.

Slowly, as if she was a punctured ball gradually loosing air, Mother had deflated. On the fourth day when Phoebe came home, Mother was in bed, there was no food in the house and Aquaria was missing. She was still at kindergarten waiting to be collected; Merlin answered the phone when the call came from Aquaria's teacher. He passed it to Phoebe and later she found him in the garden, crying and pretending not to. It was only then that Phoebe told him about Dad's note.

'I think I knew he'd run from us,' Merlin had said.

Now Mother sank onto the rug. She sat gazing out at the sea, smiling slightly.

The game started. Merlin was bowling. He took long loping strides, rubbing an old tennis ball on his shorts. Noah squinted, gripping the bat in tense hands; his mouth set in a serious line. He hit the ball and ran; up to the second wicket and back again. He stopped, looked about and set off again. The ball was in the sea. Titus and Arthur were wading in to fetch it.

'It's a six,' Phoebe called out. 'You don't have to run any more, Noah.'

After a while she left them to prepare lunch. She opened the door of the bach, stood for a moment enjoying the cool and the quiet, the pleasure of being on her own.

Later, when they'd finished tea – a picnic under the tree by the bach – Aquaria, sitting between Phoebe's legs and leaning against her, asked, 'Why did Dad have to go away?'

'I don't know,' Phoebe said. The note she'd found had been short. All it had said was that he was leaving; that he loved the children but he needed to escape. He hadn't said that he loved Mother. Phoebe had noticed that. Neither had he said he would be returning someday. But then again, he hadn't said he wouldn't.

Phoebe wrapped her arms around Aquaria, wanting to hold her close and safe, just as Dad had done to her when she was little. He'd held her tightly, too, that last evening before he'd left. He'd squeezed her to him and told her that she'd be fine and that he trusted her.

'You're not like your mother, Phoebe,' Dad had said. He'd sought her out that evening, asking her to come and sit with him on the bench at the end of the garden.

'No,' she said. She knew she was not like either of her parents and did not want to be. At school, the teachers encouraged her. University, they said. You'll do well, they said. Be ambitious, they said.

Dad finished rolling his joint and lit it. He took a few deep drags and then he asked, 'D'you want…?' trying to pass the joint to her.

'No, Dad,' she protested.

He laughed. 'You'll help your mother with the little ones, won't you?'

'Yes.' Phoebe felt impatient. Sometimes he would ramble

on, say silly things. It was embarrassing.

'You can cope, run the house, the family, manage everything?' he asked. He sounded as if he was about to cry and Phoebe stood up. She didn't want to hear any more.

He looked up at her, 'Phoebe, tell me you can.'

'Yes. Of course,' she said, wanting to go.

He, too, stood up, opened his arms, put them around her. 'I love you most of all. And I trust you. You'll always be all right. You're that kind of girl.' She felt as if she were suffocating in his embrace.

When he let her go, she said, 'Night, Dad,' and left him, almost running up the path to the house, not knowing that the next day he would leave them all.

'Maybe he'll come back,' Merlin said now, starting to gather the remains of their picnic tea.

'Do you think he might?' Mother asked, looking up at Merlin as if he somehow knew the truth about Dad.

'He won't,' Phoebe wanted to say. 'He won't,' she wanted to shout. They needed to accept that he was gone; Mother most of all. But Phoebe said nothing, not wanting to inflict more hurt. And maybe, just maybe, Dad would reappear one day.

That evening, when the younger children were in bed, Phoebe went running again. It was nearly a year since Dad had left, over a year since the last time they'd been at the bach. She ran by the sea. There was still no wind, the water turned silvery dark as the sun disappeared and she saw a figure running towards her. Perhaps it was, after all, her father coming home. She slowed down, calling, 'Hello, hello.' But the words were lost; they drifted, thin and unsubstantial, into the vast unfettered horizon.

Opening her mouth to call again Phoebe saw that there was no one there; it was just her imagination. She shook the disappointment out of her head and carried on.

As night claimed the space around her, she thought, I will go on forever. I will not stop or turn back. I am running for my life. She thought of the rabbit running the night before; she remembered a neighbour saying to Dad, his voice a sneer, 'You lot – breeding like rabbits.' Feeling the strength in her thighs, the healthy pounding of her heart, she ran and ran. She thought of her father running away and she began to cry. She knew then that when the dark became too dense she would turn back; she could not run from her family before they were ready for her to go.

Polly's Day

Polly struggles out of confusing dreams, as she has done every dawn since Jack left, and waits for the pictures in her head to clarify. She lies on her back as panic and loss recedes, calming herself by listing the chores that need doing. She rolls over into the empty half of the bed and tries to sleep again. Next time she wakes, it's bright morning and she can hear her children in the next room. Allowing herself a moment of yearning, she pictures Jack as they sat together, not quite embracing, on the day he went to war. She prays for his safe return, murmuring to a God she doesn't believe in but needs to talk to. She feels swollen with all the things she never said to Jack and wished she had. Now he's gone, she speaks to him constantly.

She remembers one evening when she was a child, in her grandmother's home… It was night, but the grown-ups were still up. Polly heard their voices coming from the kitchen and saw the faint glow of light through the open door of the bedroom. She lay listening to the breathing of Mabel next to her and the snuffling of Georgie in his cot. Polly wanted to call for Mum, to tell her she couldn't sleep and ask for some hot milk, but they didn't like it when she did that. Last time Auntie Opal came and told her not to bother her mother when she'd so much else to worry about. Auntie Opal spits when she talks and her breath smells like something's gone bad in her mouth.

'Mum,' Polly called, nevertheless, trying to make her voice loud enough for her mother to hear, but not so loud as to wake her younger brother and sister. There was no reply. 'Mum,' she called again and Mabel gave a little sleeping sigh. Polly lay listening, her ears straining. Before they came to live here, it was Dad who would come in the evenings bringing her comfort and tucking her in.

She heard the kitchen door bang open and the slow deep voice of Uncle Artie saying 'G'night.' His heavy limping footsteps came down the hall, paused outside the children's door – Polly held her breath – and then continued on to his own room.

Polly started to tell herself a story in her head about two little princesses who live with their mum, the Queen and with their dad, who doesn't have to go and fight in Europe because he's the King. There are no uncles and aunties in the palace. There's a gran who visits, but only on Sundays. Polly was wondering if there'd be a little prince, too, and what would happen next...

When Polly woke it was morning. Georgie's cot was empty. Mum always fetched him early to feed him. Mabel was still sleeping and Polly shook her. 'Time to get up,' she said.

In the kitchen Polly laid out the porridge spoons and poured milk into the big blue jug, trying not to spill. She fetched the butter from the pantry and put the jars of honey and jam on the table. When she helped, Gran was kind to her. Gran was old and sometimes her legs hurt. 'I've done too much,' she'd say, sitting with a cup of tea and her feet up on a stool. Gran was Dad's mum. In the parlour was a photo of her when she was younger and Grandpa was alive. The whole family were there, Dad and Uncle Simon sitting in the front, Gran smiling with a baby on her knee that would become Artie. Auntie Opal, the eldest child, was standing at the back with Grandpa.

'Thank you for your help, Polly,' Gran said now as they all sat down for breakfast. Mum settled Georgie in his pram then poured the tea.

'Two sons at war. I never thought I'd say it but now I thank God Artie is the way he is.' Gran sighed as she took her cup. Polly wasn't glad that Artie was the way he was, coming into their room sometimes and feeling under the bedclothes, saying, 'Have you a nice kiss for your favourite uncle.'

'I want to go home, to where we used to live,' Polly said on the way to school. Georgie was in his pram. Mabel and Polly were holding hands and walking beside Mum carefully, as they'd been taught to.

'This is our home, now, with Gran.'

'But I don't like it,' Polly said.

Mum stopped and looked at Polly. 'We have to stay here till Dad returns.'

'What if he never comes back?'

Mum bent her head and carried on pushing the pram. The terrible thing was, the shaming thing was that she was crying. Polly had made her cry.

The memory presses on Polly and she almost gasps. She calls to the children, 'Time to get up.' When she's dressed herself, she helps the youngest one, Angela, her little daughter. She stokes the fire back into life, pours water into the big black kettle and stirs milk and oats into the porridge pan. She sets it on the range and goes out, bucket in hand, to unlock the hen house and feed the chooks. Stephen comes with her and feels for eggs. There are four.

'One for each of us,' says Stephen. Polly wonders how much of Jack he can remember. It's been two years; he was four, Duncan nearly three and Angela a baby. A wave of longing for the time before the war stops her as they walk back to the house. She stands, breathless, absorbs the moment and waits for her strength to return.

Later, when she's taken Stephen to school, Polly prepares for the half hour walk to visit her mother, her gran, uncle and aunt who still live in the house that Polly escaped from when she married. Polly envies Mabel, living in the city, single and earning her own money.

Polly goes into the kitchen carrying Angela, pushing Duncan in front of her. Gran is in the easy chair, her feet on the stool, her legs dark in their support stockings. She's holding a cup of tea and grunts when she sees Polly.

'So you decided to come and see us.'

Polly says nothing. She can hear the sound of wood being chopped. It's Uncle Artie, in the garden, pretending to be useful as the only man about the place. The logs will be misshapen and the yard full of dry sawdust.

'Come and live with us,' Mum had said when Jack was getting ready to leave. 'Then you won't be lonely.'

'No,' Polly said.

'We'd like you to,' Mum insisted. Polly shook her head and shivered.

Mum sniffed and Polly put her arms round her. 'I can't,' she said, unable to explain and her mother incapable of understanding. She thought about Jack never coming back and of Stephen, Duncan and Angela trapped in her childhood home. She wondered if her mother ever felt that she would have liked to leave her mother-in-law's house, if she'd missed the life she'd led before her war.

'Can we have some cake?' Duncan asks now, standing in front of his great grandmother, watching her, his eyes big and solemn.

Gran smiles at last. 'That one is so like your father, Polly,' she says. 'Not that you remember him.' She sniffs.

Polly can remember him. She closes her eyes and sees him lifting her up onto his shoulder, she sees him smiling, she sees him kissing Mum goodbye, his hand on her tummy where Georgie was growing. Such a long time ago. Most of all Polly remembers that day when instead of Mum with Mabel and Georgie in his pram, Auntie Opal came to fetch Polly from school. Her face was red and blotchy and she wouldn't talk to Polly, though she held tightly onto her hand. Every now and then, they stopped and Auntie Opal pulled her hankie from her sleeve and blew her nose. Polly wondered what she'd done wrong. Perhaps Uncle Artie had told them about when she bit his finger to stop him. Auntie Opal pulled at Polly and made her walk too fast.

Mum was in the kitchen. She was crying like she had been on the way to school, only worse. Gran looked up as Polly came in; her eyes were red and her face all wobbly. But it was Uncle Artie who said it, 'Your dad's dead. Killed. In action.'

Polly ran outside and all around the house. She didn't know what else to do, she couldn't keep still and she needed the horrid feeling to go. 'What if he never comes back?' she'd said that morning. 'What if he never comes back?'

'He never came back,' Polly whispers now, softly so that Gran won't hear. Mum comes into the kitchen.

'We've had a letter from Georgie,' she says. She's smiling. 'Have you heard from Jack?' she asks and Polly shakes her head. She tries to stop herself feeling that it's a competition. Who will survive, Polly's husband or her brother: her mother's son?

'The sacrifice those boys make,' Gran says, sucking tea between her teeth. 'All to keep us safe and make the world a better place.'

'Yes,' says Polly and changes the subject. 'I brought you some pickles,' she says, putting the jar on the table. She made them herself from the abundance in her garden.

'You are a wonder, dear, the way you cope,' Mum says, accusing, wanting to tug Polly back into the extended family. She'd be glad if Jack never... but Polly shakes her head, stops the thought from finishing. 'Can the children have some cake?' she asks and watches as Mum clucks over her grandchildren.

At last it's time to leave. 'I must fetch Stephen from school,' Polly says. Mum, Artie and Opal come to the road and watch as she walks away, pushing Angela, while Duncan pretends to be a soldier. With a stick as a gun, he chases an unseen enemy and then stops, bending down and looking round. Polly calls to him to hurry up.

When they arrive home, Polly opens the door to the mailbox and sees a letter. Overwhelmed with gladness, she pulls it out. 'Oh,' she's disappointed. 'It's from Auntie Mabel,' she says in a bright voice.

When the children are in bed and the evening chores done, Polly sits and talks to Jack in her head, tells him of her day and how she loves him. When she can't stand the pain any longer, she goes to the end of the garden, far away from the house so that the children can't hear her. 'I hate war,' she shouts over and over till the tears come. She leans against the trunk of the old apple tree and cries for herself, for her husband and for their children. She imagines Jack, sacrificed to make the world a better place, and starts to laugh. What a silly idea. Twenty-one years after the end of the Great War that would end all wars, the whole world started fighting again.

My Father Talked
to my Silent Mother

Jill wonders now how that summer seemed to last for ever and yet also went suddenly from being crisp hopeful spring to sad damp autumn. That summer when she was fourteen and her brothers, Duncan and Andrew, were thirteen and eleven and growing apart. At the beginning they had been little boys and by the end Duncan was much taller than Jill, with long awkward legs, gangly-wristed arms and big knobbly hands that he seemed to want to hide. That summer they had all wanted to hide.

Now Jill is a mother and a wife herself and Ted, her husband, is behaving as once her father had done. She stands at the kitchen window, looking at her son and daughter. They are out in the scrubby grass of the bach, not quite playing together – they are becoming too old for that – but mooching, Natalie with a book, Luke with the old broken-stringed racket and a clutch of yellowing tennis balls. Jill wonders if they feel now as she did then and she gasps, trying to release the tightness in her throat.

It was finding the story in the magazine that made her swallow; remembering that long ago summer while living in this summer. She reads the opening sentences:

'*Through all those final hot angry months, my father talked to my mother. She said nothing.*'

Jill sighs. The story makes the father sound so reasonable. He arguing, the mother silent. Jill continues to read, '*My mother's lips were closed and straight, refusing to open for him.*'

Jill closes her eyes, thinks of her mother all those years ago, in this bach, in this kitchen, her lips straight, her back straight, marshalling silence as if it were a weapon. Her father sitting at the table, drumming his fingers on the even wood of its surface, frowning, frustration in the deep crease of his forehead and in the way his body tautened as if it wanted to move, but couldn't. Teenage Jill, sitting outside on the step by the door, leaning against the brick wall, feeling the stored-in heat of the sun on her back, kept as still as she could. She watched her father's irritable fingers and blamed her mother.

They all blamed Mum, the boys as well, although they never talked about it; not properly. One Sunday, the three of them had been in the boat with Duncan at the helm. Andrew hadn't responded quickly enough when they went to tack and the two brothers started to argue. When Jill thought the shouting was finished, Andrew said, 'There's a boy in my class whose parents are getting divorced. I'm going to divorce you, Duncan.'

'Only married people can divorce,' Duncan said, his

voice thick with scorn. There was silence as they sailed back, all of them, it seemed to Jill, wanting to be at the bach as soon as possible, as if their presence was needed to keep their parents from moving too far, too irrevocably, apart. As they were approaching land, Andrew said, 'Mum should tell Dad that she wants him here all the time.'

'He can't,' Duncan said. 'He has to work. He can only come for the weekends.' He moved the tiller, the boat came to a stop and he jumped out, grabbed the painter and stood, his back straight, looking up into the sky. 'It's not his fault,' he said urgently, emphasising the 'his', almost hissing it out.

'All parents argue,' Jill had said to Duncan that evening as they sat on the jetty in the growing dark, looking out across the bay, she swinging her legs, his dangling just above the water. He didn't reply. The problem was that only their father was arguing.

'Mum,' Jill had said. It was Monday morning. Dad had left for the city and the boys were sailing. 'Yes,' said her mother, her arms in a sink full of clothes. Jill breathed in deeply, tried to stop herself from trembling. She had to ask, although it was somehow an admission that she knew there was a problem.

'Mum,' she said again and then rushed out the words, 'why don't we go home? We don't have to stay here.'

'But you children love it here. We always spend the summer at the bach.'

'We don't have to,' Jill said.

'We do,' her mother said and Jill had sighed softly, listening to the angry slop of water in the sink.

We did, Jill thinks, so many years later. We had to stay. Mum needed that time to decide. Now Jill's watching as Luke throws a ball into the air and hits it with a big angry gesture. The ball bounces and heads towards the water. Luke runs after it and Natalie looks up vaguely. Natalie blames her, Jill thinks, although nothing has been said. Luke is just confused.

She picks up the magazine story and reads, '*While Father watched, Mother turned her back, stiff and accusing in its pale lacy blouse. I could see the sharp lines of her shoulder blades and hear the finality of her silence.*'

Jill's phone rings and she answers it, knowing it's her husband, Ted, wanting forgiveness.

'Well?' he says. It's hard, very hard, to convey with silence how she's feeling when Ted can only listen to the absence of words.

Jill wishes that Ted could see her accusing back in its blue T-shirt and know what it was telling him, although she thinks that 'pale lacy blouse' is a better image: more dismissive.

'We'll talk at the weekend,' she says, meaning that they won't talk, but that he should hear what she is saying nonetheless. She wonders if her father ever knew what her mother was telling him with her silence. Jill uses her thumb to disconnect and snaps her phone shut. Mum, she says in her head, I'm sorry I thought it was you at fault.

In the magazine story, promises fill the night, blown through the house by a hot strong wind which begs, '*forgive me, forgive me,*' which says, '*I'll change, I'll change,*' and, '*never again, never again.*'

In reality, it had been Jill's father, not the wind, promising to change. They hadn't known then, as children in that long summer, waiting for resolution, waiting for their mother to talk to him again, take him in, make them into a family again, what their father had been doing, had done so often. Even when suddenly it was over and they were back in the city, at school and he was gone and the house was for sale, there was no explanation. Just, 'Your father and I can no longer live together,' their mother told them, stiff and formal. End of discussion, she was saying as she stood in front of them, clasping her hands together, looking above their heads, her eyes like stones in her hard dry face. They moved to a smaller place. 'But we still have the bach,' Mum said. 'That at least is mine.'

Now the bach belongs to Jill and because she is a teacher, she can bring the children here for the long summer holidays, just as her mother had done.

Jill leans on the bench, tired from thinking. She wonders if her mother, too, grew tired that summer as she struggled to make the decision, to separate or not, to forgive or not. Jill wishes she had talked to her mother about that summer. A surge of anger sweeps through her. Jill knows now that it was not, strictly, her mother's fault that her marriage became troubled. Although she has long ceased blaming her, Jill realises, nonetheless, it was her mother who, finally, ended it. She turns to the section in the magazine story that describes her mother (and herself).

Jill reads, '*She could no longer speak. The man had taken*

the words and used them up. Taken their meaning and turned it around, so all that was left was an eloquent silence.'

She puts down the magazine and wonders: Is it a mistake to stay so quiet? Did her mother have no more to say, or was she punishing her father by refusing to argue? Jill remembers the pain of gradually learning, partly from what others said, partly from visits to her father, why her mother had been so silently angry. And now here she is, years later, dealing with her own husband's continuing infidelity.

The first time Jill forgave him. She and Ted had cried together. He promised, 'Never again. Please don't leave me. I will always love you.' The second time she became distant, removed from emotion. He had cried, not she.

'Because of the children, I'll stay with you,' Jill had said. 'But you must give up other women. You must.'

Ted had promised, 'Never again, never again.'

Jill's mother had been alive then, but very ill. Jill had sat by her hospital bed and waited for the right moment to talk to her, to talk about marriage. 'Mum,' she wanted to say, 'tell me about that summer and how you felt.' 'Should I leave Ted?' she wanted to ask. But when her mother woke and Jill looked at the bleak frightened face and held the cold dry hand, the words withered. She clenched her lips together, knowing that her mother was dying and there was no more to be said.

Now, Jill goes outside, taking a basket of washing to hang on the line. Natalie raises her book and starts to read.

'Nat,' Jill says when she's finished and clothes are flapping in the slight breeze, 'shall we take the boat out this afternoon?'

'Whatever,' Natalie mumbles and turns a page.

Jill feels like crying. She wants to sit by Natalie. She wants to take her in her arms and reassure her. 'I love you and everything will be fine,' she wants to say. But this is not the way she talks to her children. A cloud crosses the sun and Jill goes back inside and starts to prepare lunch.

Later, when they've eaten, Jill listens to Natalie and Luke squabbling as she drinks coffee and re-reads the part of the story she found most upsetting:

'Just before we left, Father told me that there was no more he could do, that he couldn't win. And I wanted so much, I wanted to say, that from all of this there must be a winner. But like my mother I said nothing, though my reasons were not hers.'

The father in the story couldn't win because while he argued, the mother refused to talk. But the child, the story's narrator, wants somebody to win. Jill wonders what she should do, what winning means and if it's relevant. She wonders if Natalie and Luke want a winner and if that would be her or Ted. It can't be both of us, she thinks.

Jill turns to the beginning of the story and reads it again. When she finishes, she rips the pages out and tears them into shreds. She wanted the story to tell her what to do, but it didn't. She's angry at what the story says and she doesn't like the last line; it's too passive, the narrator thinking not doing. It said, '*I stood by the window and watched Father go. Through the pane, I saw him walk down the path and silently away. In my imagination, I heard glass shatter as I broke it with my fist.*'

Jill thinks again of that long summer when she was fourteen. She thinks of her mother's silence and how she and her brothers felt. We needed to know, she tells herself. We needed the chance to speak about what we felt.

I will talk, Jill thinks now, I will talk to Ted and to Natalie and Luke. She thinks the decision would make her feel better, but it doesn't. She can't decide what to say. She could have shown them the story but she's destroyed it. Well, she reflects, maybe I'll tell them what it was called, '*My Father Talked to my Silent Mother*'. Although it's just a title and cannot give the whole story, it could be a start.

The Love Story of a Feckless Man

In spite of having few teeth, being small and skinny with tired eyes and sandpaper skin, Ted had been loved by many women. His full name was Edward Albert Richard Sydney Smyth. Much too long for a little man, so he'd always been called Ted. Except by his father who, until he'd died of cirrhosis of the liver, had called him Edward and by his mother, Molly, to whom he was always 'young Richard'. Richard was her brother, a bike-mad hippie. As a young man, he'd taken one acid trip too many and had spun out of life crashing a stolen Harley Davidson. Once she became pregnant with her only child, soon after her brother's death, Molly thought of the baby as Richard. But her husband wanted a son called Edward Albert and had only added Richard and then Sydney – his father-in-law's name – as a kindness to Molly and because the bottle of cheap whisky he'd drunk before registering the birth had made the name Edward Albert Richard Sydney Smyth seem glorious.

The name still surprised Ted, making him puff out when he saw it on official documents; even when they were from the Department of Courts demanding money or from Inland Revenue wanting support for one of his children. Ted had eleven of them although he was not quite thirty-five. He owed thousands of dollars to the courts, fines for various minor misdemeanours plus the cost of recovering the money when it wasn't paid. He also had to pay maintenance for four of his children. Two of them were now eighteen (not twins but close in age with different mothers) and the youngest five lived with him and his current partner, Cushla.

Ted loved Cushla; loved her long dark hair, pale skin and smoky eyes; had loved her from when he first saw her in a way that he'd never loved before; loved her when she was big in pregnancy; loved her when she was tired and cranky after childbirth; loved her even when she yelled and shrieked at him, fuelled by her sister's home-made wine and her perennial resentment at Ted's six elder children and their six ever-present and demanding mothers. He loved her when she was sick in bed, worn out by the life they were leading, unable to care for her own brood, leaving him to manage. At the end of the day he'd crawl in beside her and pull her to him, even her sour breath and clammy unwashed body didn't stop him. In spite of his wide experience, he'd never known a woman who could excite him quite like her. She made his heart beat as soft as sadness and his very bones melt with love and desire. He wanted to wrap himself round her and keep her safe forever.

The first Thursday of April was not a good day for Ted. He woke at four when the alarm went. He'd not slept well as one of his remaining teeth was hurting. He lay, one hand massaging his swollen cheek, the other stroking Cushla's bare buttock, and wondered if he could phone in sick yet again. His latest job was in a bakery and he started at five. The problem was that he'd taken so many days off since he'd started the job, a few months earlier. Either he'd been ill, or Cushla had and then Molly had had a stroke and was now in hospital, needed to be visited and couldn't help with the children, as she'd once done. So last week the manager had given him a written warning about his absences.

The tooth was throbbing hotly now and Ted decided. He wasn't in a fit state to make love to Cushla and he couldn't see the point of being at home with an aching jaw. He'd take some Panadol and go to work. As he opened the door to the bakery the tooth gave him a sharp jab that made his eyes water. Although he took another couple of pills he was slower than he should have been in the baking room. Twice one of his workmates grumbled at him. 'Hey, Ted, keep ya mind off the women and on the dough.'

Then, when he was outside rolling a cigarette during morning tea the manager called him into the office.

'Just finish my smoke, eh?' Ted asked, thinking, another effing warning coming. And I don't feel up for it. But the manager told Ted to sit down and sat himself, shuffling papers.

'I've had two missives about you, Ted. One from the courts and one from Child Maintenance. Have you had copies?'

'No,' said Ted. 'But I've just moved. We were living in

Harrow Street with Cushla's sister but it got too crowded with all the kids. Bit of er… a falling out there, so we haven't told her where we are. We've moved into my mum's place, in New Brighton. She's in hospital.'

'Right,' said the manager. 'Have a look at these.' He sighed. 'Won't leave you much after the deductions.' Ted read his name at the top of the first document, Edward Albert Richard Sydney Smyth, and made a proud smile. He winced when he saw the amount the courts wanted from his weekly wages, worse than toothache, he thought. He said 'ouch' out loud when he saw from the second document how much child support he had to pay.

'I have no option, Ted, I'll have to take both of those off your wages. Please try and work a full five days each week, for your own sake, not mine.'

'Sure,' said Ted, standing. Pompous bastard, he said in his mind and wondered whether to tell him to stick his job.

'Oh and let us have your new address and phone number, please.'

'Sure,' said Ted, not meaning it and went back to the baking room.

'Where the hell have you been?' shouted Cushla when Ted got home. He loved the raspy sound of her cigarette voice and the round red anger spots flaring at the top of her cheeks. He smiled at her and she handed him the baby, nearly a year old.

'Working,' he said, taking the baby and putting out a hand to stroke Cushla's thin arm.

'Don't touch me,' she said, pushing away the hand. 'You must have finished very late if you've come straight from work.' She leant back against the kitchen table, aggressively lifting her shoulders and rolling a thin joint. She looked up at him, her eyes narrowed as she licked the paper and with two deft fingers finished the process. She lit up, sucking on the cigarette as if making love to it and Ted smiled.

'There was a big order today. And we were slow, my fault, sore mouth,' he said and giving his tooth a gentle poke with his tongue realised that the pain had gone.

'I wanted to go out, I wanted you to have the kids. I dunno if I can be bothered now.' Cushla exhaled a long stream of smoke, pulled out a chair and sat on it. She gave the joint to Ted, sighed and scratched at a sore on her knee, pulling up the silky material of her skirt as she did so. Ted could see the beckoning blue veins in her thigh and realised that she was wearing dress-up clothes.

'Where were you going? Visiting a lover?' he asked, joking and passing the joint back to Cushla.

'Yes,' she said and Ted felt his heart flip in his thin chest.

'Don't be silly,' he said, waiting for her reply.

'Not a lover, but it is a date. Another man asked me out.'

'How'd you meet him?' Ted felt breathless. He put down the baby who started to grizzle, took his tobacco tin out of his pocket and opened it.

'At work.' Cushla had a Saturday job at the Pak'n Save in the city centre.

'Tell the truth,' said Ted and he put his hand under Cushla's chin and smiled into her face.

'Is the truth, he's after me and why wouldn't I be interested? He's a manager, single, can offer me a lot better life than I've got now. I'm fed up with being poor, having a dosser as a partner, nowhere to live and always being bloody pregnant. Why didn't your stupid mother tell you how babies were made?' Cushla started to cry and the baby joined in.

'Mummy, Daddy,' came a loud yell from the doorway and the kitchen was full of children with dripping noses and demanding voices.

'I've got to go and visit Ma,' Ted said later after the children had been fed jam sandwiches and watered down coke and were now arranged in front of the TV.

'OK,' said Cushla, and Ted, hearing her tiredness and resignation, put his arms round her and held her to him, rocking her gently. 'I'll make it up to you, later. You don't need another lover,' he whispered and nibbled the top of her ear.

'I don't need you as a lover,' she said. Ted ignored her.

Cushla was sitting in the kitchen when he got back. She'd redone her make-up and her hair looked brushed and shiny. He could smell the muskiness of her special occasion scent.

'I've put all the kids to bed,' she said. 'We've got to talk.'
'What about?'
'Our life.'

Ted sighed, sat down and took out his tobacco tin. How

to tell Cushla that Molly was much better and would be coming home soon so they'd have to move yet again; the house wasn't big enough for all of them. How to tell Cushla that he'd have to leave his job as it wasn't worth working with all that money being deducted. How to tell Cushla that he loved her, adored her and everything was all worthwhile when he came home to her. This last bit he could do.

Cushla shrugged.

'Shall we make another baby?' asked Ted. Cushla looked at him, shaking her head.

'Are you serious?' she asked and then added, 'You are, aren't you?'

'Of course. We could start now. You're the only woman for me.'

'So why were there so many more before me?'

'Just practising.'

'Ted, you're such a … an idiot. We don't need more mouths to feed.' Cushla had softened a bit, was almost smiling.

'It'd be the last. The final one, a round…' Ted stopped, he shouldn't say 'a round dozen' given that the first six where not Cushla's. 'A round half dozen.'

'No,' said Cushla, raising her eyebrows and stiffening her mouth; it was clear she'd understood what he'd nearly said. 'No more sex until you sort our life out. And no more children ever. And now I am going.' And she stood up and was out of the door before Ted could stop her.

She wasn't back by the time Ted went to bed, so he couldn't tell her about his job or his mother's return. He tossed and turned in bed, missing Cushla, only falling properly asleep an hour before the alarm went.

When he woke and realised that Cushla was not there, Ted sat up in bed rubbing his eyes. He'd have to call work and tell them he couldn't make it. He'd say Cushla had left and he had to look after the children. Then they'd sack him. Good.

She came back when the children were sitting at the kitchen table drinking weak tea and eating stale biscuits Ted had found in a tin. The baby was on his knee, holding a bottle to her mouth with both hands. Ted heard Cushla come in and go into the room they were using as a bedroom, heard her moving around, probably changing her clothes, he thought. The children went on eating, looking at each other with round eyes and then the middle one said, 'Where's Mummy been?'

'Staying with a friend,' said Ted, 'but she's back now.' Cushla came into the kitchen; she was wearing jeans and a too-big sweatshirt. She was pale, with skin as translucent as fairy's wings, and hands, drooping from their sleeves, as fragile as love. Ted wanted to take her in his arms and delicately stroke her until she was his again, wanted to kiss warmth back into her. He swallowed. She looked at him, her eyes expressionless and Ted, for the first time in many years, wanted to cry.

Ted wheeled the pushchair bumpily along the sand. And then came to a stop. The baby was asleep and the toddler had found some shells to play with. Cushla had said nothing at first after her return and then had asked Ted to take the eldest to school and the younger ones for a walk on the beach.

'I need to be alone,' she'd said.

Ted sat cross-legged on the sand, a hand rocking the pushchair to keep the baby asleep. He stared out to sea only vaguely aware of the murmur of the toddler talking to himself as he dug in the sand and stamped on shells. Maybe, Ted thought, I should wade out into that cold water until I die. No job, debts too large to deal with, no real home and Cushla no longer wants me, may even have been unfaithful to me. Oh and my tooth has started to hurt again.

'Hey, penny for them.' Ted looked up. Cushla was standing next to him. He stood, tried smiling at her.

She shook her head. 'You're not forgiven yet.'

'I'm not forgiven! You're the one who's been out all night.'

'Yes and I did have a few drinks with that guy.' Cushla gave a half smile. 'And then I went to see my sister. See if we could get to being friends again. And I stayed with her.'

'And will you see him again?'

'Only at work.'

'So it's over.'

'It never started, Ted.' Cushla sighed. 'And I'm back now.'

The first Friday of April turned out to be a good day for Ted; once the children were asleep, that is. It was then that he went to bed with Cushla and made love to her as sweetly and as strongly as he knew how. It was as if it were both the first time they'd been together and the last time they'd be able to, all wrapped up in the tangle of their bodies. And as she lay smiling in his arms Cushla said, 'I don't know why I love you, you feckless little man, but I do.'

'That's a good word, Cushla, feckless. What does it mean?' Ted asked, his voice slurred and sleepy with satiation, his hand resting damply between Cushla's thighs.

'It means... it means Edward Albert Richard Sydney Smyth or for short, Ted.' Cushla's words were thin with sleep. She closed her eyes.

And to Ted's delight, the baby that made his round dozen was born on the first day of the next New Year.

Escaping the Warm-blooded

Eric sometimes wondered how he'd come to be married. He'd look at Anna as she worked in the kitchen, or lay in the bath or read a book. He'd focus on the sinewy bend of her neck, on the cold sheen of the skin on her thighs, on her shiny, metallic-looking hair, on the confident veins in her efficient hands. It was her way of slicing through life, of getting things done that had first attracted him. That and her lack of emotion.

'What I like about you, Anna,' he'd said to her soon after they'd started to date, 'is that you don't seem human.' Eric saw that she'd taken it as a compliment, which was what he'd intended. She reminded him of the goldfish he kept in a tank, undemanding, nice to look at and, in a cold, strange, uninvolved way, exciting to touch. He thought of her as similar to Cleo, his pet snake and most constant companion.

Anna was a receptionist for a large IT corporation that had bought the company where Eric worked as a specialist in Artificial Intelligence. She'd started the job straight from school and by the time she was twenty-five was renowned for her competence, quick thinking, lack of humour and devotion to the firm. Management valued her because she wasted no time in idle chatter. Staff arriving late would scurry past her desk trying to avoid the accusing stare that would follow the momentary raising of her eyes to the clock above the entrance. Nobody dared to leave early. Visiting salesmen would quiver as she questioned them; clients with complaints would decrease their demands after a short session with Anna.

Eric had noticed none of this at first. He came to work early, left late, talked to few and made no friends. A week of seminars featuring AI brought Eric and Anna together. Anna was the co-ordinator and on the Friday afternoon as she stood behind the reception desk, nodding goodbye to the taxi loads of departing delegates, Eric recognised and was attracted to the coldness of her farewells. He looked at her as if for the first time, which in a way it was, as till now he'd seen her merely as the person who monitored ingress and egress to the building.

'Would you join me for a drink this evening?' he asked, surprising himself.

'No, I can't.' She turned, engaged in dealing with end-of-seminar paperwork.

'Just to thank you for all the effort you've put into managing this conference.' He came closer to the desk and she looked up. She stared at him, her eyes cool and appraising. Then the tip of her tongue slid briefly out of her mouth, thin like a little grass snake, and she said, 'Just as a thank you. In that case, yes.'

They found they enjoyed each other's company and started to meet two or three times a week. They'd sit for an hour or so in a wine bar not far from where they worked. They didn't drink more than one, maybe two glasses each, and then would go home, separately. He told her all about Artificial Intelligence. Some of those in the field thought it significant that human intelligence was shaped by emotion and that researchers into the artificial variety needed to consider that. 'I don't,' he told her. 'For me the point of AI is that you can, you must in fact, disassociate from the messiness of people. Artificial Intelligence is superior to human intelligence because it's purer.' She understood and agreed. He learnt about her reputation as the woman who controlled reception and admired her even more. She hadn't taken a holiday for years; she was worried about what would happen while she was away. He could see her point.

After a month, Eric began to consider sex. He wondered how Anna would react if he touched or tried to kiss her. He didn't find the idea particularly appealing; it was more that it seemed to be what he ought to be doing. Finally, he asked her. It seemed the obvious way to discover what Anna thought about the issue and he chastised himself for spending several days almost – but not quite – agonising on whether or not to approach her sexually. Another example of the messiness of human emotion, he told himself and I, even I, have fallen prey to it.

He told Anna this. 'You see all I needed to do was to ask you what you thought about sex in general and with me in particular,' he concluded.

'Of course,' said Anna. 'I'm not a virgin. I've not had a lot of experience, though. I think it's overrated but it can be, er, pleasant.'

'So, would you like to join me in such an activity?'

'I suppose we should try and see if we like it,' Anna replied calmly. 'You can come round to my flat this weekend.'

Eric had never been there but Anna had described it. It was new, had two bedrooms, was furnished with modern furniture and no fuss. He liked the sound of it. 'Righto,' he said as he looked at his watch. 'Time for home now, though. I'm glad we've cleared up that item.'

Anna said that she'd prepare a meal on Saturday night. Eric wondered whether to take flowers, or a box of chocolates, even both. He decided against such gifts. Far too romantic: unnecessary really. He'd said he'd bring a bottle of wine and Anna had told him what she was planning to cook so that he could choose the right match. It was to be lamb chops, grilled with tomato and mushroom, served with sautéed potatoes and green beans.

'Nourishing, but easy to make. The potatoes will add a bit of luxury. I do think people get far too extravagant when it comes to entertaining with food,' she'd added and Eric agreed. After all, the meeting was to see if they enjoyed sex together, not an excuse for Anna to exercise her culinary skills.

Eric thought Anna's flat was perfect. In the open plan living room was a small three piece suite, very plain, no cushions; a square dining table and four chairs; one sparsely stocked bookshelf and in the corner a PC on a desk. It was very neat, very clean, very tidy. The kitchen was white tiled and spotless, no unnecessary bits and pieces anywhere. The one concession to ornamentation was a spider plant in a big blue pot. It looked healthy and well fed. Eric approved.

After they'd each drunk a glass of wine, Anna served the food. When it was eaten, Eric helped her clear away and load the dishwasher. There was a quarter bottle of wine left.

'We could leave that till afterwards, if you like,' Anna said. Eric nodded assent and Anna showed him the bathroom and her bedroom. She undressed, folding each item of clothing as she did so and when she was naked, she climbed into bed and covered herself with the duvet. Eric had managed to take off his shoes and socks and was unbuttoning his shirt. He found Anna's stare unnerving and he turned his back and took off his trousers and then his underpants. He joined her under the duvet. The two of them lay on their backs, staring up at the ceiling, silent. He reached out and took her hand in his.

'You do have a condom, don't you?' Anna asked.

'Yes,' said Eric and sat up to take his wallet out of his trouser pocket. He removed the packet he'd purchased that morning, opened it and put it on the bedside table ready for later. Just at the moment, there was nothing large enough to fill a condom. He turned and started to kiss Anna. Her lips were cold and dry, but he found them arousing and as he moved his hand onto her breast was pleased to find that he was becoming excited.

Once the act was over and they'd dozed together in bed

for a little while, Anna said, 'I enjoyed that. Do you want to use the bathroom first?'

Eric told Anna that he, too, had found pleasure in their coupling and after they'd both showered and had decided that they didn't want to drink the wine left in the bottle, Anna saw Eric to the door.

'So,' said Eric as he was leaving, 'shall we do it again? Make it a regular event?'

'Why not?' Anna asked.

A few months later management told Anna that she must take a holiday, at least two weeks away from work and there was to be no discussion on the matter. So she asked Eric if he'd like to go away with her.

'Where?' asked Eric.

'Quite,' said Anna. 'I don't really like holidays.'

'I suppose we could just stay at home for the duration,' Eric suggested.

'And do what?'

'I could work,' said Eric. 'I could bring my PC round to your place and we could both work.'

During this fortnight Eric, who lived in a small studio apartment, moved temporarily into Anna's flat, taking over the second bedroom as his study. It was towards the end of the second week that Anna proposed.

'We get on well,' she said. 'We agree on almost everything. We appreciate the same things. We feel the same about sex and its place in life. We're alike. Perhaps we should marry.'

Eric looked up from the notes he was making in response

to a scholarly article on AI. He was surprised. He said nothing for a bit, just looked at Anna, at her bland expression and her smooth, dry skin.

'I thought you didn't approve of emotional stuff,' he said finally.

'What's emotion to do with it? It's a practical thing. We could sell both our places, buy something a little bit bigger. And it would stop my parents bothering me about when I'm going to introduce them to their future son-in-law.'

Eric thought for a bit more. He'd not planned on marrying; but then he'd not planned not to, either. It would have some advantages. Less housework to do, sharing meals would save time and money. Yes, he thought, why not. 'Why not?' he said out loud. 'But I'd have to bring the fish to live with us, and Cleo of course.'

This was almost the start of their first row. Anna had never been to Eric's studio. There seemed little point. Her place was bigger and she was the better cook.

'But we don't like pets,' she said now.

'We don't like fluffy pets.' Eric put down his pen. 'Cats, dogs, that sort of thing. You can't really object to fish. They just swim around. They don't make a mess.'

'I suppose they don't,' said Anna, thoughtfully. 'I read somewhere that women masturbate with them,' she added as if commenting on the weather.

Eric frowned. 'And in any case, you've got a spider plant.'

'Hardly a pet. You can't compare a plant to a snake.'

'Cleo is no trouble. She stays in her vivarium most of the time. I only let her out from time to time and then under

83

supervision. I'll introduce you to her, you'll like her.'

'All right. Take me to meet her and the fish and if I think I can live with them, we'll get married. Though I have to say I don't see the need for pets.'

'It's not a need. I enjoy the company of fish and snakes.' Eric picked up his pen and bent to scrutinise the paper he was annotating. He looked up again. 'I once asked my parents if I could keep a cockroach as a pet.'

'And?'

'They refused.'

Anna met the fish and the snake.

'They remind me of you,' Eric told her. Anna said that she could accept them into her home. Shortly afterwards Eric found himself married and the co-owner of a flat with three bedrooms, one of which became his study.

'Why do we need the third one?' he asked and Anna said, 'More space. And just in case.'

'In case of what?'

'We ever have overnight visitors.'

Cleo lived in the study. Often when he was working, Eric would let her out of her vivarium and handle her. He enjoyed the cool dryness of her skin and the slight thrill of fear that she generated in him as she wrapped herself round his arm or thigh or, once or twice, his neck. Anna took over the feeding of the fish. She developed an affinity for them and was happy to spend time watching them moving round their tank when Eric was occupied with his work.

Then one evening, Anna came into his study and stood looking down at him and at Cleo, curled in his lap.

'I've bad news, Eric,' she said. 'I'm pregnant.'

'What?' said Eric as Cleo slithered down his leg and across the floor. 'You can't be. We didn't want this. We didn't plan for this.' This is why I should not have married, Eric thought, as he leaned over, picked Cleo up and put her back in the vivarium.

'Nonetheless, I am.'

'I don't want to know this,' Eric said. 'It's horribly messy.'

'Yes,' said Anna. 'We have to decide. Have it or an abortion.'

'An abortion,' said Eric. 'No question about it.'

'That would normally have been my reaction,' said Anna. She frowned. 'But there's something that's stopping me accepting it as the solution.'

'Not emotion, I hope.'

'I think it is. I think I'm having an emotional response.' Anna stared at Eric, her normally placid face creased with anxiety. He stared back.

'If being pregnant has done this to you; the sooner you get it stopped, the better,' Eric said finally and turned back to his PC.

Anna dithered. She acted out of character; refused to make the decision to have the abortion. Eric waited, sure that eventually she would make the right choice. But time passed and Anna was still pregnant. Eric found the idea of an embryo growing in her body distasteful. One Friday night he logged onto a website that showed pictures of babies from conception onward. The child inside Anna was a fish, he thought, a blind fish.

One Saturday, Anna miscarried. When it started she called a taxi and travelled on her own to hospital. She phoned later to tell Eric that the pregnancy was over.

'Good,' he said. 'You're well rid of it.'

When she came home the next day she was quiet and went straight to bed. Eric had to cook his own evening meal. This was not why he married, he told himself. He went into the living room and looked at his goldfish swimming around in their tank. They no longer appealed to him, reminding him of the mess that had lately been inside Anna.

Time passed. The pregnancy was not mentioned, but still made its presence felt in that Eric could no longer bear the sight of his fish, nor could he make love to Anna for fear that she would conceive again. Although she said nothing directly, Eric became aware that she would have liked their sex life to resume. When she went to bed, Eric stayed up, working, often with Cleo curled round one of his limbs.

One late evening as she slithered over his body, Eric shut down his PC, wrapped the snake round his shoulders and went into the living room. He reached his hand into the tank and taking the fish out one by one, he fed them to Cleo. After he put her back in her vivarium, he went to the bedroom very tempted to wake Anna and make passionate love to her. But he resisted.

The next morning he woke remembering the events of the night before. As he sat up, Anna, already fully clothed, came back into the bedroom.

'Where are the fish?' she asked.

'My fish. My fish, you mean.'

'Whatever. They've gone.'

'I know. I disposed of them.'

'How?'

'My business.' Eric looked up at Anna and into her eyes; they were as yellow and as cold as the eyes of goldfish. But they were also angry. 'Tell me what you've done with them,' she said.

Eric thought that if he told her she'd do something drastic, kill Cleo, something like that. In that moment, he knew he should never have married. He continued to look at his wife and she continued to stare at him.

'Are you going to tell me what you did with them?' she asked eventually.

'No, Anna, I'm not. And if you don't leave now you'll be late for work.'

'So will you.'

'I'm taking a day off. Tell them I won't be in today,' he said.

Anna turned and left the room. She could not bear the idea of being late, Eric knew. He heard the jingle of her keys as she picked them up from their allotted place on the hall table, then the slam of the front door, followed by the quick taps of her feet as she ran down the stairs. He lay back on the bed and rubbed his eyes. Anna was human, he thought, he should never have thought of her as otherwise. He stretched, rose from his bed, went into his study, opened the vivarium, reached in and picked up Cleo. He wrapped her round his arm, went back into the bedroom, and lay down. He stroked her skin and let her slither over his body, pushing with her head as if looking for something. She slid over his shoulder and slowly she wrapped herself round his neck and started to squeeze it with a gentle pressure. He tried to pull her off, to loosen her hold, but she responded by increasing her grip. His last thought as Cleo tightened herself round his neck was, 'I am dying. I am being crushed to death by a snake.' He found it immensely exciting.

Remembering Peter

'*Shakespeare throws as much light on the Marx brothers as do the Marx brothers on Shakespeare,*' Peter said. 'That's the first line of the book I'm writing.'

'That's good.' Sue was looking at him, the tall thin lanky body, the limp beige badly cut hair, the pale defensive eyes. They never stopped moving: flicking around the room like lizards' tongues, eager to trap each unwary morsel.

He waved his hands, gesturing. 'I haven't got any further.' He looked down at his cup, the remains of the coffee now cold. He scanned the room as if absorbing its features: the tables each with a row of chairs on either side; the counter, empty now of food; the closed serving hatch behind it; the barred windows that gave onto the sunless basement area; the two or three patient-made pictures on the shabby paint-peeling walls. A dismal place; made worse by the smell of watery cabbage, over-cooked meat and burnt milk.

She wondered if he knew how to smile; sometimes his lips twitched at the corners and a glimmer appeared in the flatness of his eyes. He shifted in his chair, uncomfortable. In the few weeks since he'd arrived at the day hospital, he'd told her so much about himself: that he was socially awkward, never felt at ease, was most dreadfully shy. It didn't strike her as odd when he was speaking that he was articulate and able to talk about feelings, which he shouldn't have been given the picture of himself that he was painting. It was only after their conversations that she realised there was a dissonance between what he said and how he said it.

'When I left Oxford it was because I was ill. At first, I thought it was physical. A pain in my chest, I told the doctor. Inability to breathe. I was rushed to hospital. Even then I wondered if I was a fraud, lying on the stretcher with this terrible massive banging – almost audible I thought – where I imagined my heart would be. They prodded and poked, tested and x-rayed and told me there was nothing wrong. That's when they sent me to see a psychiatrist and the next term I didn't go back, I came to live in London instead.'

'I thought you thought you had a brain tumour.'

'Yes I did, later.' Peter shuffled his skinny legs in their flapping trouser, cleared his throat. 'Another ride in an ambulance. A pain in my head, so shocking that I staggered when I walked, slurred my words when I spoke. That time I was sure I was dying, nothing false or fraudulent. I still get the headaches sometimes. Terrible they are, as if heavy metal were swelling in the brain. But I've had the scans and the probings and they say there's nothing wrong.'

'But you're not sure.'

'No,' he said, his hands dancing in front of him. 'I'm not

sure that I trust doctors. They're not the ones who've felt the terrible agonies that our bodies inflict on us. How do they know?'

'Tests, machines, all that.'

'I'm not sure that they are any better. They don't have souls, how can they tell the truth?'

'Do you really think you're physically ill?' Sue asked. He didn't reply for quite a long time, but she could see that he was thinking, wondering how to answer.

'Perhaps and there again perhaps not,' he said finally.

Sue watched him, trying to imagine what it would be like to have sex with him. She frowned: the idea of kissing his mouth, of his hands on her body would not take shape. He seemed to be totally asexual. She wondered if he were a virgin, was sure he was, there'd been no mention of friends when he spoke, neither male nor female.

'I had a girlfriend once,' he said, surprising her. Again the almost smile as the eyes flicked towards her and then away. She breathed in deeply, surprised, waiting for more and she was struck, as she had been before, by his strong dry smell, as if he were made of hay.

'An experiment,' he said. 'Though I did enjoy it.' He nodded. 'While it went on, I stopped thinking about whether or not I was well. I even put on some weight.'

'How did it end?' she asked.

'The weight gain?'

'No, your... affair. The girlfriend.'

'Oh. I think she realised that I wasn't normal. She wanted to know if I thought I might marry her one day. I took too long to reply. By the time I'd thought of the answer, she'd left. She never came back. I'd see her from time to time. I tried to speak to her once, but she turned away and it was shortly after that I left university.'

It was in his first week at the centre that Sue had befriended Peter, feeling that he needed to be treated gently. He seemed to wear his feathery vulnerability like a frail cloak. The way he sat, always on the edge of his chair ready for flight, his stillness, the jerkiness of his movements and the look of surprise in his eyes when anyone spoke to him; all of these things made Sue want to protect him. She felt that he was not substantial enough to survive the heavy earnestness of the therapeutic process that this strange experimental day hospital existed to provide. But then, she thought, so few of us patients are.

Footsteps came down the corridor and a head appeared round the door. 'Peter, Sue, there you are,' it said cheerily. 'You've missed the afternoon meeting.' The door pushed open and the owner of the head came into the room and stood looking at them, hands on hips. It was James, the chief psychiatrist: short, plump, stocky, with glossy dark hair and a high colour, he radiated good health, stability, the pleasure of being sensible and the necessity of normality. Sue noticed his feet in their big soft boots, placed firmly on their floor at just the right angle from each other to hold him in solid place. She wanted to tell James that the talking she and Peter were doing was far more useful than any doctor-led therapy group. She wanted James to leave them alone. She frowned, hoping he'd notice her subtle warning, but he just put his head on one side waiting for some response.

None came. So, 'What are you two doing here anyway?' he asked.

Sue shrugged, looked at Peter.

'Ruminating,' said Peter, 'working on the task for the day: devising a motto for this place.'

'Oh,' said James, 'and have you thought of one?'

'Yes,' said Peter.

'And what is it?' James asked, his voice wary.

'Life is like a cucumber. One minute it's in your hand, the next it's up your arse.' Peter's tongue flipped out of his mouth, licked his lips, flipped back inside again so quickly Sue wasn't even sure it had happened. 'Good isn't it? A very suitable slogan for us.'

James's hands left his hips, lay dangling by his side, big and meaty. 'Er, not sure, Peter, that it's the right saying for a therapeutic community.'

'No?' Peter said. 'I would have thought it highly appropriate. I think Sue and I, indeed all of us "patients" here,' – (he put inverted commas round the word patients, making it sound like an artifice, a word that should not be used) – 'us "patients" here have had numerous cucumber-like experiences, not necessarily up the arse but painful in their invasion.'

'Right,' said James, dismissive in his tone, signifying that Peter was far from right and more likely to be wrong. Sue felt a slight fizzing in her veins that she recognised as anger. She wanted to tell James what she thought of him, and how much she despised his certainty, his sanity, his unassailable conviction that given a choice all of the inmates in this establishment would opt for the kind of life he lived instead of their own. She wanted to shout at James and tell him that he was an emotional imbecile. She wanted to stand up and yell at him to go. Instead, she gave him a false smile and watched him misinterpret it. James smiled back, conspirator like, saying silently, she knew, 'Bad luck Sue, being stuck with Peter and his boringly mad pronouncements.' Then he cleared his throat.

'You shouldn't be here, you know, house rules, canteen only at meal times. You'd better get along. Let the kitchen staff get the place ready for tea.'

'He said nothing to you, then?' James asked, his lips pressed plumply together. Sue noticed that they were a little damp. She wished that she had a tissue to pass him so that he could wipe them.

'I wouldn't say he said nothing.' Sue knew how imprecision irked James. She watched, nearly smiling, as he frowned and then sighed.

'What did he say?'

'He's told me a great deal about himself.'

James raised his eyebrows. Although Peter was often pressed to speak about himself in the therapy groups, he didn't respond in a way that the staff found satisfactory, Sue knew. He was irreverent, enigmatic, given to obscure observations that made James re-cross his legs and suck in his breath. She watched now as James rubbed his chin with thick fingers, controlling his anger.

'What I wanted to know is if he said anything about not coming back to the hospital, since he hasn't been here all week,' James said, each word clearly enunciated, clipped and cross.

Sue said nothing for a bit, just looked at James and his round sensible face. For a moment she felt sorry for him, locked in the world of the scrupulously sane. She shook her head. How could someone like James imagine he could penetrate the uneasy shifting uncertainty of Peter.

'You think he may have attempted suicide, don't you?' she asked eventually. James had started to blink rapidly. How frustrating his life must be, thought Sue, all us ridiculous patients with our mental illnesses refusing to benefit from the wisdom, experience and training of him and his colleagues.

He dismissed her comment with a slight shake of his head. 'One of the staff will have to visit him. Find out what's going on,' he said, but he was no longer talking to her. Sue sat down as James strode away. She closed her eyes. Forget one of the staff: she wanted to visit Peter. He had told her where he lived, not the address, but almost. If she could recall the steady, slender tone of his voice, hear it in her head, she was sure she could remember exactly what he had said.

'It's on the top floor of a corner house. I was attracted by the name of the street, "Riddle Rise" and by the landlady who is small and very Hungarian.'

Right, thought Sue, that should be enough to find him.

Sue wondered if her knock had been too soft. She was raising her fist for another attempt when the door opened. There was Peter, standing almost motionless, tall and pale; his face impassive.

'Can I come in?' Sue asked and he moved back into the room. She followed, looking round: a single bed, a chair, a chest of drawers and in the far corner a small oven and a sink. One mug lay upside down on the draining board. There were a few books on the shelves under the dormer window and nothing on the round coffee table except an empty sheet of thin paper and a cheap biro.

Peter sat on the bed, carefully, his knees together, arms by his side with his palms pressed down on the coverlet. He said nothing, didn't ask why she was there.

'They've all been worried about you, thought you'd tried to kill yourself,' Sue said, realising she wanted to cry.

'Me?' he asked, unsurprised. 'No... no,' he said. Sue waited for a wry comment, an observation that revealed Peter's unusual connection with the world. None came.

'So where've you been?'

'I've been writing the next line of my book.'

'Your book?'

'Yes. I've got it now. It reads, "*Shakespeare throws as much light on the Marx brothers as do the Marx brothers on Shakespeare. But for an understanding of cucumbers we need to read Chekov.*"'

Sue stared at Peter and he stared back. He was strangely still, his eyes unmoving. Then he spoke, 'That's it. The last line. I can't manage any more.'

The Homecoming

It seemed to Rose, thinking of the time before she, as she put it, became herself, that life was dark and struggling: father absent, mother sad and distracted. And England at war.

The first time she knew who she was, she was standing between Grandma and Grandpa, wearing the coat made from an old pair of her father's trousers.

In the last month of summer Mummy had sat listening to the wireless, turning the handle of the sewing machine, guiding the material under the needle. Then she would stop, look critically at the garment, call to Rose to come over. She would stand and be fitted with a sleeve, a collar, some part of the unfinished coat.

When it had become real and not just mysterious sets of brown tweed attached to each other in strange ways, Mummy told Rose to open the sewing tin. Rose put in her finger and touched buckles, pieces of ribbon, little fancies of lace. 'Oooh,' she said.

'Careful,' Mummy smiled, though she still had her cross

look. 'Look, a lovely piece of braid. We'll add that to the coat. It was on a jacket of mine that's too shabby now.' Mummy's sigh made Rose wonder what she'd done wrong.

'Help me choose the buttons.'

'Those,' said Rose, pointing to some big shiny ones.

'No,' Mummy said. 'Not red. We need ones that go with brown.'

'I like those,' said Rose, bold for a moment, wanting to wear the bright colour of the buttons.

'No,' Mummy sighed again. 'Maybe later I'll put them on a dress for you. These match your coat.' Mummy picked out some small, dark-looking, leathery buttons that made Rose feel sad. Her lip trembled. Mummy shook her head. 'No need for tears,' she said.

When the coat was finished, Rose wanted so much to wear it, in spite of its buttons.

'It's for winter,' said Mummy.

'Winter,' Rose repeated. 'Is it winter after tea?'

Mummy almost smiled. 'Oh Rose,' she said, making her watery laughing sound.

Rose wore the coat for the first time on the day she realised who she was. Years later Rose could recall the moment: that understanding that she was a unique individual, separate and different from everybody else. I am me she thought as she stood between her grandparents. This is my grandma, that is my grandpa. I am wearing my new coat. Soon we'll go out. I am me, here in the house where I live with my mummy. I have a daddy, but he is being a soldier. I am me. Rose remembered almost shuddering with the realisation that she was who she was. The looking down at her shoes and her thick stockings, the feeling of the wool of her gloves against her skin, the waiting between her grandparents for her mother to appear; the murmur of talk from the grown-ups as they stood, tall on either side of her in the dark wooded hall: all of it part of who she was and the way she was.

When her children asked what it was like during the war, Rose answered in different ways, depending on how she was feeling. In truth, she did not know. She couldn't differentiate between the war and her time as a pre-school child when she'd believed that everybody lived in a dark house with a preoccupied mother, that fathers were absent. Life, she understood, meant food and clothes rationing. It meant queuing at the butcher, the greengrocers, the fishmonger, the baker. It meant black curtains at the windows at night and sitting with adults who talked in hushed voices about missing men, men who'd died, men who'd 'never be the same again'.

I should have been spoiled, Rose would ponder, the only grandchild to two sets of grandparents. Her father's parents seemed to Rose old and strangely remote. She called them formally, Grandmother and Grandfather. She remembered the dry herby smell of their house, the squeak of clean linoleum in the hall, the soft deep tick of the clock on the mantelpiece that told her to move slowly, talk quietly.

Grandmother poured tea and passed bread, covered with

pale pink almost non-existent jam, followed by thin slices of cake.

'I'll give you the recipe, dear,' she said to Mummy. 'It doesn't use much in the way of rations.'

Grandfather spoke to her twice, once when they arrived, 'How's my favourite girl?' Then he picked Rose up, kissed her with his moustache, as grey and bristly as the scrubbing brush that lay in the scullery bucket at home. He put her down and let out a little puff of air between his teeth. When they left, he kissed her again, saying, 'You look after Mummy till Daddy gets back.' He stood at the door, next to Grandmother and waved as Rose and Mummy walked up the path and down the road. By the time they turned the corner, the door was shut.

Between the time of arriving and the relief of leaving, Rose sat in a big squashy chair in the drawing room listening to Mummy and Grandmother. They sighed when Daddy was mentioned; Stanley they called him. They shook their heads when they spoke of rationing. Their voices went low when they talked of other families and their losses.

When tea was over Grandmother took a book from the shelf. 'Here Rose, you look at this while Mummy and I do the dishes. Look after it mind, it was your daddy's when he was little.'

Rose opened the book with scared fingers; worried she might make a mark or, worse, tear the pages. But she liked the pictures with their faded colours and the strange black squiggles that Mummy said were words. Rose pretended to read the squiggles, telling herself a story under her breath, not wanting to disturb Grandfather. His newspaper was folded over his face, rising and falling to the rhythm of the noise his nose was making and which Mummy said was called snoring.

Each visit was, as Rose remembered, just like the one the week before.

Rose was happiest with Grandma and Grandpa, Mummy's parents, and with Kitty and Dulcie, her aunts. She loved to run into their house, calling 'I'm here'. One of them would pick her up and swirl her round. She remembered arriving like this even before she could make sentences, only just able to walk. She remembered stumbling ahead of Mummy and calling some nonsense word; the swoosh as she was raised into the air, that made a tickle start in her throat and spread over her body; the giddy feel as she was swung about; calling 'more' when she was put down and raising her arms for a repeat.

Rose knelt on a chair at the kitchen table, helping Mummy make the cake. Daddy would be home tomorrow and they'd been saving their rations. Rose didn't remember Daddy. She squeezed her eyes shut to see if she could find a picture in her mind.

There were photographs of him, one in a frame, more in an album. Rose liked to look at the photos. They started when Mummy was a girl. In the middle was a whole page with Mummy and Daddy together, smiling. Mummy looked different: not just younger, but fuller, as if she had a secret she mustn't tell. Daddy had wavy hair and a big moustache that looked soft, not bristly like Grandfather's. The last pages in the album were of the wedding, Mummy sitting down and wearing a frothy frock and Daddy next to her, being important. There were her grandparents, Kitty and Dulcie in their bridesmaid dresses, groups of people that Rose didn't know. Then there were two blank pages and no more pictures, as if life was no longer worth recording once the wedding was over.

So Rose knew what Daddy looked like, but it wasn't the same as remembering him. In the photos he didn't move and had no colours, only black and white. Tomorrow he would be here, having tea at this table. Rose opened her eyes and gave the cake a big stir.

'That's enough,' said Mummy, 'it's ready now.' She poured the mixture into the greased tin. 'Is it all for Daddy?' Rose asked.

'No. Some for you and me and some to take for Grandfather and Grandmother.' Mummy put the cake in the oven and stood up, arching her back, rubbing it with the back of one hand. All day Mummy had been busy; every room had been cleaned; floors swept, lino washed, wood polished and windows rubbed with newspaper soaked in vinegar and water. She'd made the big bed in her room with clean sheets and tided up the wardrobe and the chest of drawers.

'Won't it be nice with Daddy home?' Mummy asked. But Rose saw the little flicky bits at the corners of her eyes and the way her mouth turned into a line.

Next day Mummy took Rose to Grandpa and Grandma while she went to meet Daddy. After lunch, they'd come to fetch Rose.

'Will Daddy stay long?' Rose asked Grandpa as she knelt on the path and dug with her trowel, helping with the vegetable plot.

'What a question, girly, of course. He's home for good now the war's over.'

'But what if...' Rose stopped, lifted her trowel. Something made her feel it wasn't the right sort of question. She shouldn't be asking what would happen if she didn't like Daddy living with them.

'Maybe I should stay with you and Grandma,' Rose said instead, peering up at Grandpa. He frowned, leant on his spade and then looked down at Rose.

'Rose love, it'll be nice to have your daddy home.' He sighed. 'Come on now, Grandma's made soup for our lunch.'

Rose, back in the garden, lying on the lawn, looking up into the sky and singing a little song, heard Mummy calling. 'Rose, come and say hello.' Rose looked up. Mummy was standing by the back door. Next to her was a man: not tall. Almost the same height as Mummy. His hair was short and looked nearly red with the sun shining on it. He waved. That's not my daddy. My daddy doesn't look like that. My daddy is big and tall and has black hair. She rolled over, humming.

'Rose,' called Mummy and Rose ignored her. 'ROSE,' Mummy called in big letters. Rose closed her eyes. She heard the footsteps on the path. They were strong and not her mummy's. Rose squished her eyes even tighter shut and let the humming get louder. Then came his voice, quite low and with a question in it. Rose could feel him leaning over her, blocking out the sun and making her shiver. His hand came down and touched hers. His skin felt dry and his fingers were hard and bony and could hurt. Rose wondered whether to start crying and sniffed in preparation. She'd stopped humming when she'd felt the cold of his shadow pass over her. 'Come child,' he said, gripping her hand.

'No,' said Rose, pulling away. She felt invaded. She felt panic. 'Grandpa,' she screamed. 'It's no good, Eunice,' the man said. 'She doesn't want to know me.' His voice was sad, lower than before. Rose opened her eyes and looked up at him. He smiled, but Rose didn't like it. She wrapped herself into a ball and began to cry.

Grandpa came and gathered her into his safe, solid arms. He took her into the parlour, stroking her hair until the sobbing stopped. When she'd quietened, he said, 'Now, girly, it's hard for you. Someone you don't know coming along. But it's your daddy, who loves you. Some little girls aren't lucky enough to have a daddy at home. Now will you be good for us?'

'Yes, Grandpa,' said Rose. But she wasn't sure. Worse still, with the arrival of this stranger in her life, she was no longer sure of who she really was.

Cheryl and Me

Her enormous breasts jiggled around under the silky blouse like two fat babies clinging to her chest. I was mesmerised. What would she look like naked? Could she lie face down? How did they feel? She clasped our hands tightly, Cheryl on one side and me on the other and made us walk even faster, making the babies bounce and skip. I caught Cheryl's eye and made a face, leering upwards.

When Cheryl started to giggle, she turned to her.

'What's so funny?'

'Don't know.' Cheryl stopped laughing and her face went pale and pinched.

My little sister Cheryl is sickly and frail and gets frightened easily and that's why I look after her. I'm only a year older but ever since I can remember, I've had to take charge.

'Do you want to go to the swings?'

'Don't mind.' Cheryl's lips quivered, she'd be crying next.

'Course we want to,' I said and gave Cheryl a look. I

control her with looks; she knows what they mean. This look said don't cry, don't make trouble, agree to whatever she says.

I try not to make trouble, because enough trouble's caught up with us anyway. But sometimes I can't help it, like making Cheryl laugh when I shouldn't.

'You'd better be good girls, with your gran sick, we don't want naughtiness.'

'No, Miss Bates,' I said and the sadness hit me again. But I never cry, no point in it. It just makes your face wet.

We'd seen Miss Bates at church on Sundays, she was always there at the front wearing a big hat and singing with a loud voice, but we'd never been close to her before. She'd come to our house that morning and Aunt Moira opened the door when the bell rang.

'Good morning, I'm Miss Bates. The vicar tells me Mrs Wright is sick. I've come to see if I can help.'

Moira didn't know what to say; she just stared at Miss Bates. Moira's slow and simple, her nose and eyes were all red from crying, her dress was stained and her hair was sticking up because she hadn't brushed it. She'd forgotten to give us breakfast that morning so I'd cooked pancakes and Cheryl and me were eating them with our fingers. We were still in our pyjamas and the kitchen was messy, as the pancakes had been difficult to make.

'Can I come in, dear?' said Miss Bates and I made a face at Cheryl and went into the hallway. Aunt Moira was standing at the door and she'd started to cry again. When she saw me, Miss Bates said, 'Oh, the poor child.' She pushed past Moira and came into the house.

'It's our gran that's ill,' I told her. She went into the kitchen and said, 'Oh' again. She found a cloth and sponged our hands and faces. And then she took an apron out of her bag and started to clear up, washing the dishes, wiping the surfaces and table. She threw away the pancake mix, swept and mopped the floor. I stood in the doorway, holding Cheryl's hand. Moira stood behind us, whimpering.

'Shut up Aunt Moira,' I said and Miss Bates turned to look at me and raised her eyebrows.

'God doesn't like rude children,' she said. 'Apologise to your aunt.'

'Sorry, Aunt Moira,' I said, but when Miss Bates wasn't looking I stuck my tongue out and crossed my eyes. Cheryl giggled.

I like to make Cheryl laugh; I like the sound she makes. She's often unhappy because she can't remember Momma who died when we were small. I was only three but I can see Momma in my mind, I can hear her singing and feel her smiling, but Cheryl can't. Sometimes Gran takes us to our momma's grave and that makes Cheryl sad. We take flowers for her and I talk to her in my head but not out loud, I don't want Cheryl and Gran to hear, they'd think it was stupid talking to a dead person who's not even really there. Once I got cross with Momma and told her she shouldn't have left us. That was when our dad had gone away and I was worrying about Cheryl.

After Momma died, Dad went funny. Sometimes he

didn't get up in the mornings and we could hear him snoring. The first time we went into his room and I shook him and he shouted and snorted and turned over, but he didn't wake up. At first it was scary but then we stopped minding and in the mornings when he slept I'd tell Cheryl stories and help her dress and tickle her to make her laugh. One time she was laughing so loud it woke Dad and he came into our room and shouted, 'Stop making that noise, stop it, stop it.' And he took my hairbrush and hit me on my legs and it hurt worse than when a wasp stung me. Then he hit Cheryl, but not so hard. Her face went all red and angry and her mouth opened wide ready for a good big wail. I signalled to her not to cry, I thought it might make Dad even crosser. But he saw that she was trembling and he dropped the brush and knelt down and cuddled us both and said, 'I'm so sorry, so sorry. My poor little girls.' And then he cried, our dad, a big man, crying. Of course, that made Cheryl cry too. And he tightened his arms round us and pulled us closer. I didn't like him cuddling, he smelt sour and stale, his eyes were sore and watery and his face was scratchy. He'd slept in his clothes too, and they were dirty and crumpled. I used to have to tell him to change his clothes and remind him to buy food and things like that.

'My ma's sick,' wailed Aunt Moira, 'I can't look after these children, they're too much trouble. What can I do, what can I do?'

Miss Bates took off her apron and patted Aunt Moira's arm. 'I'll get them dressed and take them out, let you have a break.'

'We can dress ourselves,' I said.

'Then go and do it,' she said and Cheryl and I went up to our bedroom.

'Stupid cow,' I said. 'Who does she think she is, bossing us around? Stupid Moira, she can't even look after herself.'

'Stupid cow, stupid Moira, stupid cow, stupid Moira,' chanted Cheryl.

Then we heard Gran calling from her room, not a call really, more of a moan, but we knew she wanted something and we tiptoed in. She was lying in the big bed, her small head like a little bird on the pillow. She had no teeth in and when she breathed it sounded like snoring.

The room was dark as the curtains were closed and it smelt of old lady, illness, medicine, stale body and pee.

'Give me a drink, pet,' she whispered and I took the glass and lifted her head, but she could hardly swallow the water and some spilt on her chin and on the bedclothes. Cheryl was shaking and clenching her fists. 'Will you be better soon?' she asked.

'Yes, my pet, come and give Gran a kiss.' And Cheryl moved to the bed slowly, kissed the crumply damp face quickly and ran out of the room. She didn't want Gran to see that she found this revolting. I felt the sadness coming in, so I started to breathe deeply.

The doorbell rang again and Aunt Moira came up the stairs with a nurse who'd come to see to Gran. Behind her was Miss Bates who said to me, 'Still in pyjamas?' So I went back to my bedroom and we dressed and while I brushed Cheryl's hair, I told her a story about two princesses that lived in a glass palace and wore silk dresses and flowers and jewels. But before I could get to the best bit about marrying the handsome princes, Miss Bates came in.

'If you're ready girls, I'll take you to the swings.'

'Can we say goodbye to Gran first?' I asked.

We loved our gran. She sometimes used to come to our house when we lived with Dad. Then she'd clean up and cook food that made the house smell homey and tell us stories. We'd sit in the kitchen, all warm and cosy and eat chicken and for pudding, apple pie with cream and it would feel like we were a real family, like the ones in our storybooks. We'd have a long deep bath and Gran would dry us with clean towels that she'd washed earlier. And our bedroom would smell of ironing and fresh laundry and she'd tuck in our bedclothes and kiss us goodnight and sweet dreams.

Then sometimes she'd go and talk to Dad and she'd get cross with him. And we would hear the twisty sound of him opening the whisky bottle. Cheryl would creep into my bed and I'd hold her tight while we listened to the angry chink of Dad's teeth against the glass. The voices would get louder, the door would slam and the day would be spoilt.

Gran brought us to live with her when Dad left us. We haven't seen him since, Gran says he's sick and when he's better he'll come for us but when I ask her when, her eyes go misty and she turns away. And now she's ill. She's been in bed for nearly a week.

But we couldn't say goodbye to Gran.

'The nurse is with her and we're not going for long,' Miss

Bates said. And that's when she took us out and hurried us down the street to the park where the swings are.

'Who needs pushing?' she asked.

'Cheryl does, but I can do it myself.' I climbed onto a swing and I worked and worked till I couldn't go any higher or any faster and the sky was moving back and forward above me and I thought I was flying and free like a bird. I put my head back and called, 'Look at me.' And I swung and swung until I felt dizzy.

Then Cheryl and I played on the slide while Miss Bates sat on a bench.

'Do you like her?' Cheryl whispered. I thought for a bit.

'I think she's better than Aunt Moira.'

'Everybody's better than her, she's funny in the head.'

'And she's not nice,' I said. Aunt Moira pinches us when Gran isn't looking. Once she sat and ate a whole bag of toffees, making a nasty sucking noise and dribbling all the time and she didn't give us one. Each time she took a toffee she threw the wrapping papers on the floor and when she'd finished, she said, 'Pick up all those papers or I'll tell Ma you put them there.' So she was a liar too. And she was clumsy. When she broke Gran's best salad bowl, she told Gran that I'd done it.

'I didn't. Gran, I didn't,' I said. It was the last time I felt like crying. But Gran believed Moira; we loved our gran and she loved us, but she loved Moira the best.

'It's because she's her youngest child and is handicapped and needs Gran even more than we do,' I'd told Cheryl when Gran was cross with us because Moira told her we'd been teasing her.

Miss Bates called, 'It's time for lunch, I'd better take you home.'

'There'll be no lunch, Gran's too ill and Aunt Moira always makes a mess if she tries to cook.'

Miss Bates took our hands. 'Would you like to go to a café, instead?' I opened my eyes wide at Cheryl. That told her that maybe Miss Bates was not too bad.

'Yes please, yes please.' Cheryl started to skip.

We all chose fish and chips and Cheryl and I had Coke. Then we had ice cream for pudding. Miss Bates had a pot of tea and she asked us why we lived with our gran and where were our mum and dad.

'Our momma died and our dad had to go away. When he comes back we'll live with him,' I told her.

'But we do like living with our gran, except for Aunt Moira, she's a loony,' said Cheryl.

'That's not a kind thing to say about an unfortunate person like her,' said Miss Bates quite crossly and Cheryl looked down, biting her lips, trying not to cry. But then Miss Bates put her hand on Cheryl's head and stroked her hair. She sighed and shook her head. I knew she was feeling sorry for Cheryl and me and I don't like that.

'We're alright with our gran.'

'I'm sure you are, dear. And I'd better get you two back to her.' She was talking in a cheery voice but I could tell she was worrying, too.

When we came into our street there was an ambulance parked outside the house. I gripped Miss Bates' hand tighter; I was shivering. We could hear Moira crying before we reached our front door. When we went into the kitchen, I wanted to tell her to shut up. But our doctor was sitting at the table writing something and Miss Bates was there; they'd think I was rude, so I just mouthed it at Cheryl, pretending I felt fine and I rolled my eyes to make her laugh. But she didn't laugh; she was shaking too and her face was a funny greeny colour.

'It's Ma,' said Moira, sobbing, her face was rubbery, wet and snotty. 'She's going to die.'

The doctor looked up at Miss Bates. 'I'm having her hospitalised, I'm sorry but there's no hope; it's a matter of days at the most.'

And Cheryl said, 'I want my gran, I want her better.' And her eyes were big and her lips thin and tight.

'I'll always look after you,' I told her, but I couldn't think of anything to do or say that would take away that frozen look. Miss Bates was standing between us. She bent and put her arms round us, one round Cheryl and one round me.

'Poor little mites,' she said and hugged us to her bosoms. I could feel them now, soft and squashy as she pressed our heads into their warmth. But now I didn't think they were funny, I didn't want to know how they felt. I wanted her to go and leave me with Cheryl so I could cuddle her and tell her stories and make believe that we were lucky girls and all was well. Miss Bates was holding me so tight I could hardly breathe and my nose and mouth were crushed against the silky blouse. I started to choke and then I was crying; clinging to her and crying and I couldn't stop.

Sweet Susie

The blonde woman said it. A university lecturer, Martin told me, called Jude. She was laughing and talking, her loud posh voice all round vowels and brittle consonants. One of them said it – she said it – but they all thought it. Thought I was young, stupid, conventional and why was Martin with me; thought I was too stupid to know what they were thinking.

'A bird in a cage, Martin,' she said. 'A canary and she wears fluffy slippers.' Martin said nothing. He didn't talk much when doing business, only said what he had to.

'And so domesticated.' Her voice went silky on the 'so' and 'domesticated' came out like peas from a pea-shooter. She turned as I came into the room. She took a drag on the joint and passed it to Jerry, her boyfriend, though they're not a good pair; she so shiny and jangly, he quiet and shadowy.

'Tea,' I said softly. 'And biscuits.'

'Hey, Sweet Susie, come here,' Martin said and I handed round the tray of mugs, took off my apron and sat on his knee, swinging one leg till the slipper fell off. What's wrong

115

with wearing slippers? I wanted to ask, but didn't. They'd only laugh at me. She, Jude, was wearing long pale green suede boots, silk shorts and a tight top that revealed the shape of her tits. She smiled. She reached forward and took a biscuit and then nibbled it as she leant back. Showing off her body. Tart, for all her plummy accent, she's a tart. And old. At least thirty. And I was only seventeen and the one Martin had chosen.

The room was dark. Martin's flat was a basement and he kept the curtains closed, even during the day. I'd tried to stop that. I'd be up and doing the housework while he was still in bed. I'd yank the curtains open and get out the vacuum cleaner I'd brought with me and I'd dust and polish. I even cleaned the windows and bought pot plants. Martin often worked until two or three in the morning and unless he had an early visitor, he'd sleep till lunchtime when I'd cook for him. After eating he'd go into the living room and wait for his calls. He'd sit in his big armchair watching afternoon TV and sometimes he'd call me.

'Hey Sweet Susie, close the curtains, I don' wan' the whole world seeing me working.' And I'd stop whatever I was doing; washing the kitchen floor, ironing or tidying and I'd come and do what he asked.

But I'd complain. 'It's not good sitting in the dark, Mart.' He'd laugh. 'Do you want plod peering in watching me rolling joints or cutting lines?' And I'd pout and he'd say, 'Come 'ere, Susie, and be sweet to me.'

Sometimes we'd make love on the living room floor or on the armchair. He'd tell me to take my clothes off and he'd stroke my body and look at me. But he'd just undo his fly and ask me to suck him or caress him. Sometimes he came that way, but sometimes, especially if he'd had cocaine, he'd put himself inside me and go on forever, till I started to worry that I'd never get my chores done. I don't see why sex is so important. Kissing's nice. And I like being in bed with Martin, cuddling, and he's lovely when it's all over. Soft and gentle like a big baby.

We'd made love the day that Jude mentioned my slippers. Just as he'd finished, the phone rang. It was her. She asked if they could come round and Martin had said yes, but in a couple of hours. He was expecting visitors. He said it so she'd know what he meant. Jude and Jerry were regulars. Here at least twice a week to buy, cocaine usually and sometimes the other stuff, the dope. When he said he was expecting visitors he meant the big guys were coming to deliver the goods he sold on.

I didn't like them. I'd go in the kitchen when they came. I'd make a cake or some scones. Although I'd offer them tea I'd take it in and leave it for them. Then I'd stay out of the living room till they'd gone. They laughed at me, even more than Jude. And they were frightening. Once when I came back from shopping they were threatening Martin.

'Come on,' the really big one was saying, his voice sounding like water gurgling in a rusty pipe. 'Don't give me shit about waiting for little girlie to tell you where the money is.'

'It's true,' Martin said. His voice was thin; he was scared but not as much as you'd expect. He's been in his business

117

for years and he's used to nastiness. He said, 'Hey Susie,' when he heard me in the hall. 'Where you put that money?' I went to fetch it and gave it to him, trying not to look at the big fat knife the really big guy was holding in one hand, rubbing it with his stubby thumb. I was trying not to show that my hands were as trembly as tissues in the wind.

That morning there'd been stacks of notes – tenners, twenties, even fifties – all over the living room and I'd put them in the biscuit tin. Normally Martin's not so careless but last night he'd been drinking, which is unusual. In bed he'd smelt of mouldy biscuits, he'd been rough, which isn't like him and he'd fallen asleep before he'd finished. Most people see Martin as seedy, a drug dealer without a life, a hard man with no emotions. But I knew different. I knew he was soft and vulnerable and needed looking after. One day, when we'd saved enough, he'd give all this up. He hadn't said that, but that's what he wanted. What we wanted. And I was longing for it. I didn't like the drugs at all, wished that wasn't how he made money.

Occasionally, maybe once in two, even three years, Martin went back home to see his old mother. That's where I met him; his last visit. His elder brother was our neighbour and I knew his daughter, Tracey. She took me with her to her nanna's and Martin was there; tall, big, the best looking man I've ever seen with a secret smile and smoky eyes that kept watching me till my skin turned inside out. I badgered Tracey to take me back that evening and to leave me alone with Martin. I wanted to see what I could make him do. I sat opposite him in the kitchen while Tracey took her nanna upstairs to find some family photo or something.

He looked at me silently and I pouted and stretched my arms across the table. He laughed, taking my hands his. His skin felt gritty and his touch made me tremble. He laughed again and said, 'Come here,' and I went round and he pulled me onto his knee and we kissed. We stopped when we heard footsteps on the stairs, but I told him I'd wait for him outside. That night he told me I was beautiful and far too young for him. A few days later when he said he was going back to the city, he held me for a long time and he was almost crying.

'I'll miss you, little girl,' he said. 'So fresh, you are, so sweet.'

'You don't have to miss me,' I told him. 'I'll come with you.'

'No, you're a different life I might have had,' he said and touched my face. 'Goodbye, Sweet Susie.' But I wrote down his address and I said I'd see him soon.

It's true I was shocked at first, not the drugs so much as the state of his flat; dirty, no food in the kitchen, sheets on the bed that hadn't been washed for months and that stale metallic smell that I never got rid of. But I came to see him most weekends and I made his flat more comfy and one day when we were lying in bed Martin nuzzled my face in a way that made me know I loved him.

'One day, Sweet Susie, we'll have a proper home. A garden for you and lots of clean light rooms with views of mountains and sky.' He laughed.

'Till then I could live here.'

'No, I was joking, you'd hate living with me full-time,' he said.

'No I won't, I'll look after you, I'd love it.'

'No, Susie, no,' he said, but I knew he didn't mean it and the next Friday I came with all my things. My canary in his cage and all my clothes and bits and pieces I needed for housekeeping. My brother, Ted, brought me in his car; we'd left my mother waving at the gate. I'd told her I was going to share a flat with a friend. When we arrived, Ted helped me unload. Martin looked at the cases and boxes and he started to laugh. Then he went and sat down and didn't help at all. I didn't mind, though my brother thought it was strange. 'Don't say anything to Ma,' I told him and he shrugged. When he'd gone Martin made love to me and afterwards he said, 'So I've got you all to myself, have I Sweet Susie?' And he smiled and fell asleep, so I knew I'd been right in moving in.

It hasn't been easy, though. Every evening people coming, cluttering up the living room, sprawling on the sofa like aggressive cushions and wanting tea and such, giving me stringy looks as if I was the maid, not talking to me, but I can almost hear them thinking 'what's Martin doing with her?' Just because I don't take drugs and don't lead the silly lives they all do. I kept thinking how it was going to be worth it, though, with the money I was putting in the bank for Martin and me. He made a lot and didn't spend much – he hardly ever went out and never shopped. I kept thinking of the country cottage and the garden full of flowers and Martin no longer dealing.

And now it's all over. It started being over a few days ago. I came home from shopping. It was early evening. I bumped the trolley down the basement steps and stood by the front door, feeling for the key in my pocket and everything was normal. Then I opened the door. I went into the living room. My brain somersaulted in my head and my teeth went fuzzy. My insides felt as if they were fizzing out of me and my skin turned brittle and cold. Martin was in his chair and Jude was sitting on his knee. Her blonde hair was all about his face and I could hear the plucking noise of lips as they kissed. I screamed and they came stickily apart as if they'd been glued together.

'Hey, Sweet Susie,' Martin said. I screamed again. 'Stop screaming, Susie.' Martin was trying to sit up.

'I'll go,' said Jude and she stood, reached for her bag, bent her face to Martin's and walked out, saying, 'See you.' My body was shaking like ice cubes in a cocktail mixer. Martin rose and came to me and put his arms round me.

'Stop, Susie. It was only a little kiss.'

'You were with another woman,' I whispered. I felt that if I didn't hold back my voice it would jump out of my throat and throttle Martin.

'You don't own me, Sweet Susie.'

'But you're my man.'

'I think I'm my own man.'

'But Martin. I love you. You love me, don't you? You wanted me to come and be with you.'

'As I recall you just moved in one day.'

'But you want us to be together. You talked about a

proper home.' By now we were in the armchair, Martin was holding me tightly and nuzzling his nose into my face. But something wasn't right. He wasn't saying the right things. A painful hole was being dug in my chest. I was even finding breathing difficult.

'Let's fuck,' said Martin.

'No,' I said, because it wasn't right. 'You do want to be with me, Martin, don't you?'

'Sure,' he said and I let him make love to me, but the hole in my chest just grew tighter as if filling up with tears.

And then today when I came home I knew something was wrong. Heaviness was buried in the silence and there was a musky smell that wrapped itself round me. The hole in my chest burnt as I went into the bedroom and saw Jude lying quiet on top of Martin, her hair all round his face and shoulders and the sheets damp and used about them. They woke when I screamed. I went on screaming as Martin held me and Jude dressed and left. I could not stop screaming, though the sound was thinning. I felt worn out and my throat was sore.

'Stop, Susie,' Martin said again and this time I did because the effort was now too exhausting. I sat on the bed and when the phone rang Martin answered it. All he said was, 'Fine.' He put the phone down and looked up. His eyes were hazy and his skin tired. 'I'm expecting a delivery. The big guys are coming. We'll talk later.'

He went to shower and I knew what to do and was glad I'd baked a cake that morning. I walked slowly into the kitchen to prepare and then I was back in the bedroom watching Martin dress, my hand behind my back. When he'd finished I went to him and stabbed him in the heart with my best knife. The one I keep sharp and gleaming. Martin frowned at me and I yanked the knife out hard and did it again. This time something bubbled from his nose, he snorted a little and then he fell. I knelt down and heard the last breath gasping from his mouth. I waited a little but I knew he was dead. There was a big thick stain on his shirt from the blood that had oozed from his chest. I pulled out the knife, stood up and went into the kitchen to clean it.

When the men come, I'll say Martin's out and I'll give them tea. I'll ask the really big one to cut the cake. I'll give him the knife so that his fingerprints are on it. They'll go finally when Martin doesn't come back. I'll put the knife back in its wound. Then I'll call the police and tell them what happened. How the big guys murdered Martin. And they won't suspect me, Sweet Susie, a stupid little girl, too young, too conventional for this kind of life.

Playing with Clay

He'd forgotten again. Another year he'd missed Mother's birthday. 'Silly old bat,' he mouthed and then flushing with the guilt of it, shuffled into his studio where he slapped his arms round his body trying to warm up. He stamped up and down in his thinning flappy slippers. He took a handful of clay and flipped it onto the long loose legs of his latest sculpture. 'Hm' he called it. 'Hm,' he said and giggled. All his pieces were called 'Hm' when he started them. All were tall and spindly with drooping attitudes and weak attenuated limbs; creatures created from his aching indifference. Or so some fatuous art critic had once described them. '*Trevor Monk's aching indifference to the human condition allows him to spawn pieces combining terrifying power with an equally terrifying powerlessness.*'

Trevor slapped on the clay, squashing it with his fingers, giggling at the silliness of the art world. Then he remembered Mother. 'Bugger her,' he said, emboldened by the satisfaction of playing with clay and of laughing at the idiocies of critics. They had with their words transformed the results of his obsessive need to keep his hands damply busy into internationally acclaimed money-making sculptures.

The phone rang. Trevor ignored it. He started to hum, squeezing clay between his fingers, letting it dribble in globs onto the thin limbs of his latest 'Hm'. Looks like me, he thought, scratching his stubbly chin with the back of a clay-covered hand. All his pieces looked like him. Tall, thin, knobbly. Smelly, too, he thought, raising his arm and sniffing at the sweat-crusty patch under his arm. Might have a wash tonight. Celebrate Mother's birthday with a bath. Maybe.

Trevor was rich. He'd been born forty-two years earlier to a wealthy father who'd died soon after and a small fuzzy-haired mother with unhappy eyes, whose main interest was indulging her only son. Then he'd accidentally made money as a sculptor but spent little of it. He lived in a cold decaying cottage with no bathroom – to have a bath meant heating water and filling the tub that hung on a hook in the outhouse. The cottage was at the end of a long rutted track and Trevor left it occasionally in his old van. He paid no rent as the cottage was his mother's and the phone, his only luxury, was there at her insistence and she paid for it.

At midday he went into the kitchen where he rinsed a saucepan that had been sitting in the sink, opened a packet of soup, which he heated and then ate straight from the pan, dipping the end of a stale loaf of bread into it and sucking the results hungrily into his mouth. The soup tasted vaguely of clay and of the remains of tinned stew that had been the last food cooked in the pan. Trevor smiled. I am disgusting, quite disgusting. The thought gave him a warm, comforting feeling. He dipped his hand into the remains of his lunch, rubbing the last bits onto his fingers, which he licked with voracious pleasure.

This time when the phone rang he answered it. 'Hello, M-m-mother,' he said.

'It's not Mother,' came an amused female voice.

'Oh, s-s-s-sorry,' said Trevor. 'Er, then who?'

'Anne Spright. You remember me, don't you? I'm interviewing you this afternoon. A piece I'm writing for *Art* magazine. Just checking that it's still alright before I set off.'

'Yes, um, I'm er, expecting you,' Trevor lied.

'Good, I'll be there about three.'

'Um, s-see you then.' Trevor put the phone down. Bugger, how could he have forgotten that a tart was coming? He looked at his fingers, covered with clay and soup, looked down at his shabby trousers, stained and dusty and at his yellow-skinned, grimy feet in their holey slippers. He smiled: all part of the Trevor Monk image.

'Er, this is m-m-my s-s-s-studio,' said Trevor, watching as his visitor walked round the room, stepping carefully to avoid treading on the lumps of clay, old newspapers, dusty rags and other debris that covered the floor. Her nose was wrinkled, against the rich aroma of her host and his home or in general distaste at the mess and muddle that surrounded her, Trevor couldn't tell. She nodded as if to reassure herself. She was youngish and pretty. She had an athletic body and moved with assurance.

Shame I hadn't bothered to wash, thought Trevor, I

might have tried to chat her up. But he felt no regrets. It was fifteen years since he'd had a sexual encounter. Not long after he'd begun to become famous, with money he didn't need that he'd made from selling sculptures at a show, he'd taken a woman, a fellow artist, another but less successful exhibitor at the same show, away for a weekend.

He'd been hoping to fall in love with her. She'd been beautiful and eager. He remembered her face, swollen with lust, her long hair brushing his chest, as they'd made love in the afternoon. He remembered the curtain fluttering in a slight wind, letting shafts of sun light her body as she came. He remembered her hot moans, her damp apple-smooth skin, her avocado smell that grew stronger with her arousal. And he remembered watching it all from inside his head, wondering, as he'd done each time he made love, why he felt nothing. Intense pleasure, yes; physical delight, the exquisite dancing of his nerve ends as he moved towards orgasm and the final ecstasy of letting go. But no emotion, no sense of closeness to the person who engendered this momentary physical rapture, no desire to hold her to him and tell her how precious she was. Rather the reverse. A need, in spite of post-coital tiredness, to leave the bed, to shower, clean himself and find somewhere to be on his own.

She'd been angry with him, that woman. Though she'd said nothing, he was aware of her disappointment, her frustration that all her beauty, her sexuality, her hard emotional work was useless, had not had the effect she'd been anticipating. But she's not nearly as disappointed as I am, he'd thought, realising again that he was unable not only to love but to feel anything positive towards another human, unless, of course lust counted as positive. My wish is that one day I'll be able to enjoy those mushy flutterings that other people seem to feel.

'Hm,' he said now, watching Anne the journalist as she looked round the studio.

'Don't you find it difficult, working in this mess?' she asked and Trevor was surprised by the aggression in her voice; usually journalists treated him with respect. The few that had come to the cottage had either pretended not to see the dirt and disorder or had interpreted it as an essential part of his artistic endeavour. *'The calculated and chronic chaos which Trevor Monk so strenuously sustains in his studio is a rich enigmatic source for the lean straining lines of his work much as the most rotten compost results in the growth of the sweetest fruit.'*

'I like m-m-m-mess,' he said. 'Have you s-s-s-started the interview or were you just curious?'

'Both. Do you mind if I record us?' she asked, holding up a small cassette player. 'And is there somewhere we could sit down?' She looked distastefully at the one seat in the room, an old armchair, clay-spattered, with torn upholstery and leaking stuffing. Trevor shrugged. 'The um, kitchen,' he said.

Before sitting down she wiped the seat of her chair with a tissue taken from her bag. Then she asked questions, nodding as he answered and eyeing the little red light on her recording machine. She asked about his training – he'd not been to art school but had spent years as a boy playing with clay; about how he first became interested in sculpting – he hesitated before answering this. He didn't want to say that he was indifferent to sculpture, that his interest lay merely in the delicious shivering feelings that the touch of clay engendered. Early on in his career he'd told an interviewer that he had no interest in what he produced. This had resulted in a eulogy on Trevor's humility and how this allowed him to '*manipulate his medium as it transcends itself, becoming, as if by magic, an object that has broken free both from its material and its maker.*'

He mumbled a response, culled from that very article, 'so it's s-s-sort of m-m-m-magic, s-s-s-sort of transcendental,' he finished. She frowned.

'I don't believe you,' she said and Trevor shrugged.

'OK, we'll drop it. I'd like to ask you about your personal life.' She leaned back in the chair and Trevor, seeing the push of her breasts against her blouse, was aroused. I wonder would she come to bed with me, he thought. Probably not. I'm not an attractive proposition: too thin; slack-skinned; dry sandy hair and not much of that. And just now I stink and my clothes are dusty and stained. In any case I can't be bothered. I'd rather do it to myself when she's gone. That way I can persuade her to take part in all sorts of acts she'd only agree to in my imagination.

'Well?' she said and Trevor realised that he'd not heard her question.

'Um, ask m-m-m-me again, I wasn't er, listening,' he said. She wanted to know about his early life, his parents, and then she said: 'You've never married. Have you ever had a girlfriend – or a boyfriend?'

'Yes, um, both. You must have, er, read about m-m-m-me. There's enough written.'

'Sure, but I wanted you to tell me directly.'

'OK. Then yes, I've had um, girlfriends, I've er had boyfriends, too.'

'Tell me about your first experience.'

'A friend of m-my m-m-m-mother s-s-s-seduced m-m-me.'

'Did you enjoy it?' She leant towards Trevor and he felt again the quick rise of desire for her, or at least for sex. He hesitated, how to tell about that terrible night when he was only fifteen, the mucky mixture of delight and disgust.

'Yes and no,' he said simply and she laughed. 'Anne, um, it is Anne, isn't it?' She nodded and Trevor continued. 'Would you like to er come to bed with m-m-m-me?'

'No thanks, Trevor. You disgust me. I'd like to finish this interview and go.'

'Did I frighten you?'

Anne looked at him, her head on one side. 'No, you didn't mean it. You just wanted to shock me.'

Trevor smiled at her. Just wait till you've gone, he thought, then I'll do things to you that'll make you swoon with pleasure, scream out for more.

He answered the rest of her questions and then he took her back into the studio and showed her a few of his pieces. She looked at them critically.

'Do you like them?' she asked finally.

'No,' said Trevor. 'Um, people want them, s-s-s-so I er exhibit them.'

'You know what, Trevor Monk? You're all fraud. I think your work is a sham and your life is a sham and this existential chaos is nothing but a disgusting mess because you're lazy and dirty and you've no talent at all.'

Trevor stared at her; he giggled. 'S-s-s-someone er once wrote an article that s-said just that. I um s-s-s-sold even more pieces afterwards.'

'I'm right, then. You are a fraud and you're proud of it.'

'Maybe, but um the m-m-m-mess is deliberate. I do er have a talent for m-m-m-making a m-m-mess.'

Anne smiled at him and for a slender second Trevor found himself warming to her; he breathed deeply at this slight suggestion of a good feeling for another human being.

'Time to go,' she said.

As they were walking through the cottage towards the entrance, they heard the noise of a car bumping down the track. Anne followed him to the front door and they watched as the car stopped.

'M-m-my m-m-mother,' he said as an elderly woman bustled out of the car and looked at him, her arms folded.

'Who's this?' she asked.

'It's OK,' said Anne. 'I'm going. I'm a journalist. I've been interviewing Trevor.'

Anne went to her car, opened the door, gave a wave, got in and drove away.

'Is she why my special day was forgotten?'

'No, M-m-mother. She's um only been here about an hour. I'm er very s-s-s-sorry about your birthday.' There was no point in telling her to go, explaining he wanted to be on his own, that he'd drive over later to see her. No point at all. He sighed.

'I can see you're glad to see me,' Mother said, looking at him critically. 'You need a bath. And I expect your place is in its usual mess. Why you continue to live here, I just don't know.'

'Because I like it,' he said, turning to go back into his cottage.

'In that case you'd better make the most of it,' he thought he heard Mother say and wrinkled his forehead, wondering what she meant. He sat in the kitchen while his mother clattered around, trying to clear up, moving pots and pans, boiling a kettle of water to wash dishes and talking all the while.

'Now Trevor, I'm saying this for your own good. You're my son and I love you. I know you're an artist and deserve certain indulgences but living like this is bad for you. Good thing it won't be for much longer.' Trevor closed his eyes letting the words wash over him, much as he'd done as a child, just saying 'Yes, M-m-mother' or 'No M-m-m-other' when it seemed appropriate. More than anything he wanted to be alone.

His eyes snapped open at something his mother had said. 'What?' he asked.

'So that's that. Only another few weeks,' she said.

'S-s-s-say it again. I um didn't hear you properly.'

'I've sold the cottage. To someone who wants the land for development.' She sighed. 'You don't listen to me, do you? I sign the papers tomorrow.'

'You can't. I live here. It's m-m-m-mine. Where will I go?'

'Come home to me.'

'No,' Trevor shook his head and stood up. 'No. You're m-m-m-mad.'

'Now then, Trevor, that'll do. I think you should light the boiler, have a bath before you take me out to dinner.' His mother dried her hands on a hankie she'd taken from her sleeve.

'OK,' said Trevor, feeling quite calm and when the boiler was lit, he went into his studio. He stood gazing down at the table, at the dirty coffee cups, smuts of clay, old envelopes and a cereal bowl caked in sour grey milk. He smiled and flexed his fingers, went over to his clay box, opened it and dipped both hands into it.

'Come here,' he called to his mother and when she did so, 'look out of the window,' he said. As she stood with her back to him, peering through the greasy pane, telling him that she could see nothing through such dirty glass, he came behind her, put his clay-covered hands round her neck, grasping it tighter and tighter as she spluttered and struggled.

He giggled and loosened his hands. She collapsed, coughing, her hand to her throat.

'Trevor, what are you doing?' she asked, her voice strained.

He looked at her, at the dumpy body on the dirty floor and he felt a rush of heady emotion: hate. His mother was trying to stand up. He went back to his clay box. As his mother continued to struggle into an upright position, he slapped clay onto her face and into her mouth. Moving quickly he grabbed handful after handful of clay and rubbed them onto his mother's body. 'Mmm,' she tried to complain. Trevor was full of a strange empowering energy. Soon his mother was completely covered in the thick grey substance. When she tried to push at Trevor and to remove the clay, he put one arm round her and held her tight while he pushed more of the stuff into her eyes and nostrils. He put his open palm against her clay-covered face and held it there until she stopped moving. As he let her go, she fell limply to the floor.

He continued to take handfuls of clay and build on the lump that was his mother. Humming, he turned the body as he worked. This one's not called 'Hm', he said to himself.

When he'd finished, he used the hot water to scour each room in the cottage. He left the studio to last, tidying and mopping round the mound of his latest sculpture. Then he bathed, washed his hair, shaved and dressed in clean clothes. I love mess, he said to himself, but it's best when you start from clean, when the mess spoils what's pristine.

Sitting at his scrubbed kitchen table he opened a bottle of wine and poured a glass, smiling to himself. He thought about his mother's final struggle and giggled. He took his wine into the studio and sat looking at his dead clay-covered parent. After a bit he went and knelt by the body, stroking the clay and reshaping it with both hands. I wonder what the critics will say about my new work, he thought. '*Trevor Monk's latest sculpture, entitled 'Mm', shows a radical and*

135

profound departure from his previous oeuvre. His shift from delicacy to corpulence signifies a change from humour to solemnity, showing Monk moving towards maturity. No longer playful he has, at last, become an adult, deeply immersed in the awfulness of the human condition.'

Trevor giggled, stood up, took more clay and went back to the body, adding the moist medium in thick gloopy lumps, squishing the soft gritty dampness of it into his palms, feeling the squelch of it between his fingers before plopping it onto his mother with busy hands. 'I should have done this years ago,' he said, breathing thickly with heavy pleasure.

The Sleeping Handsome

Once upon a time in a remote kingdom, a king and queen were sadder than sad because in spite of lengthy infertility treatment and numerous IVFs they had no children. So on her fortieth birthday the queen gave herself a present and that was to stop trying to get pregnant. She and the king started to enjoy their lives again; they laughed and played and made love for its own sake, not for the purposes of procreation. And lo and behold the queen conceived and the little prince when he was born was loved beyond belief not only because he had been so wanted and such a long time coming but because his parents had had such a good time creating him.

His christening was the most sumptuous affair. Nearly everyone was invited from the richest courtier to the poorest peasant. Among the guests were two of the three resident fairies. The third fairy did not receive an invitation because the king and the queen did not like him. He worked as a weather forecaster and was always predicting rain and wind, storms and tempests, even a typhoon although the kingdom wasn't in a typhoon area. It was due to the hard work of the other two fairies, both of whom also worked in the kingdom's meteorology centre, that the citizens enjoyed, on the whole, good weather, warm summers with just the right amount of rain and short but frosty winters.

As the bad fairy was the only person living in the kingdom who had not been invited, he was bitterly angry and stomped around his office in a terrible mood wondering how he could punish the king and queen for leaving him out.

Finally he thought of a plan, punched his fists upwards and shouted, 'Yes!' He rushed to the palace before the christening party was over. Everyone was having a great time. The king had ordered crates of champagne and the queen had told her cooks to spare no effort or expense in creating the most mouth-watering dishes. There was non-stop music to satisfy all tastes and the court jester was busy making everyone laugh.

When the bad fairy arrived, it was gift giving time. Each guest, from the youngest peasant to the oldest aristocrat, had given the little prince a present. The last to give their gifts were the two good fairies and the first was saying, 'I was thinking of giving great beauty to this child.' He nodded to the king and queen. 'But given his parentage he will undoubtedly be supremely handsome. So I have decided to bestow on him a quality far more useful. I hereby give this child the gift of lifelong happiness.' As he finished speaking the bad fairy rushed into the hall. 'And I give this child the gift of death. He will, on his eighteenth birthday discover the drug heroin and three days later he will die from injecting a contaminated dose.' And the bad fairy laughed an evil laugh and stealing a couple of bottles of the best champagne left the palace.

The queen turned white and the king looked grim. No one spoke. It was so quiet that you could hear the bubbles fizzing in the champagne flutes. Then the second good fairy cleared his throat, the noise echoing through the silent palace, and spoke. 'I haven't given my gift yet,' he said. 'I was going to donate long life but instead I'll provide an antidote to the bad fairy's curse. I can't reverse it completely, my powers aren't strong enough, but the prince won't die, he'll just fall into a light coma and if the right woman comes along he'll probably recover.'

The party finished after that; no one felt like eating or drinking after the disastrous events. And in any case the king and queen had taken the little prince and locked themselves in their private apartments.

The king was pacing the floor trying to think of a way of making sure that his son would never encounter heroin. In their younger days the king and queen had smoked dope and had even tried cocaine once or twice. The police in the kingdom were lenient towards the milder illegal substances and had few problems with harder stuff: as far as was known, there were no heroin users in the kingdom. Nonetheless, the king was worried. He turned to the queen, and asked, 'My dear, what shall we do?'

'There are three things that we must do,' said she. 'First we must banish the bad fairy from the kingdom.' The king ordered this done and the pressure on the two other fairies working in the meteorology centre was immediately lifted and the weather was perfect for the next eighteen years.

The second action advocated by the queen was to call the chief of police and to initiate and perpetrate a never-ending battle against all illegal drugs and their dealers in the kingdom. This annoyed some of the regular dope users, especially those older ones who'd smoked with the king and queen when they'd been a mere prince and princess, young and fun-loving. There was a lot of grumbling about people becoming middle aged and forgetting the pleasures of youth. But in general, people understood these measures and that they were to protect the future of the heir to the throne.

The queen's third recommendation was to keep the little prince safely in the palace away from any temptation. The boy grew up without the benefit of companions of his own age. He was happy, though, he'd been given this gift by the first good fairy and he had, as well as kind teachers and loving parents, plenty of toys and books, horses to ride and pets to play with.

The morning of the prince's eighteenth birthday dawned, as mornings now always did, warm and sunny and the prince woke happy, rested and eager for another wonderful day. He stretched and leant out of the window and then he showered and dressed and went for a pre-breakfast ride on his favourite horse. When he came back to the palace, breakfast was still not yet ready – the cooks were making a very special effort for this birthday meal – so he decided to explore parts of the palace he'd never visited.

Before long, he came into a large attic and there, sitting on a velvet chair, was a man he'd never seen before, smiling an enigmatic and dreamy smile. 'Hello, prince,' he said, 'come and sit by me.' And the prince did and he saw that the man was holding in his hand a syringe, rather like the ones used to inject the prince against diseases when he was a small child.

'What are you doing with that? Are you a doctor?' he asked.

'Oh, no, I'm not a doctor,' answered the bad fairy, for it was he. He'd managed, after eighteen years of travelling the world, causing bad weather wherever he could, to sneak back into the kingdom disguised as a pharmaceutical salesman. In this guise, he'd also managed to smuggle in quantities of illegal substances.

He smiled at the prince. 'I'm a magician,' he said. 'In this magic syringe is a magic potion, which will make you happier than you can imagine happiness.'

The prince laughed. 'I don't need anything like that, I'm already happy!'

'I know you are, but this will make you a different kind of happy.' And the prince was interested. He was beginning to find, after eighteen years, that happiness might be happy but it could also be a tiny little bit boring.

'OK, I'll try it, what do I have to do?' And the bad fairy showed him how to inject himself and the prince took his first shot of heroin and was astonished and delighted by its effects.

He was late for breakfast, ate little and seemed dreamy

and distracted, but still he was sweet and obedient, smiled at everyone and gave no trouble.

It was customary in the kingdom for the eighteenth birthday of the heir to the throne to be celebrated over three days, culminating in a big ball for all the citizens on the third evening. The king and queen had decided that, now he was of age, the prince should meet others of his own generation and the ball was to be the occasion for this introduction.

The prince had been looking forward very much to the ball; apart from anything else he was obsessed by sexual fantasies and was hoping to meet girls able to make these fantasies real. Had he not been given the gift of happiness by the first good fairy, he might well have been rather miserable by this time at his lack of friends and by the absence of normal adolescent sexual experiments. His encounter with heroin dulled all these emotions, replacing them with others that he wanted to feel again and again. Over the three days of his birthday celebrations he made his way to the secret attic as often as he could and took what the bad fairy had to give him.

It was the evening of the third day and the prince had dressed for the ball. He left his room and stood at the top of the stairs that led down to the great hall where the party was to be held. His parents sat on their thrones at the other end of the long room greeting guests as they arrived. Music was playing and waiters were offering champagne, the room was filling. For the first time, the prince saw groups of boys his own age and, even better, huddles of pretty girls. He felt a moment of excitement and then turned for a final visit to the attic.

The bad fairy was waiting and this time not just with heroin, but with another even more poisonous substance in the syringe. The prince took it, pinched a piece of flesh to find the vein and pushed in the needle. He began to squeeze in the intoxicating contents when something made him stop. He looked up. The bad fairy, thinking his job was done, was leaving. The prince felt a strange rushing in his ears, his eyes closed and he fell onto the satin chair, the syringe still stuck in his arm, its contents hardly used. He passed out. He'd taken enough of the poison to cause a coma.

Down in the big hall a sudden hush, a cold shiver passed through the room. The two good fairies looked up and saw the bad fairy leaving the palace, a look of triumph on his face. Sadly, the second fairy shook his head and then, gently raising his arms he sent everyone in the palace, everyone in the kingdom to sleep, including himself.

Years passed and the rest of the world forgot the remote kingdom where the people slept and the forests grew.

And then one day a young female anthropologist, a graduate student, eager for challenge, decided to try to enter the kingdom. There were rumours about an ancient people who had once lived there and she wanted to see if there was any evidence for these rumours. The way into the kingdom was difficult, thickly forested, dark and dense but she persisted and after several days of travel found herself in front of the palace.' Wow,' she said to herself, 'it looks like something out of a Walt Disney film of a fairy tale.'

A little nervously she entered the palace. It was, it seemed, full of lifelike statues, including one of a king and a queen sitting on thrones. The place was eerie, cobwebby, silent, cold and musty. But the anthropologist was persistent and making notes as she went, taking photographs and talking into her cassette recorder, she explored every corner of the palace. The last room she came to was the prince's secret attic. The door, as such doors should in fairy tales, creaked as she entered it. She saw what she thought was a statue: the sleeping prince. She touched his black curls and his lightly bearded cheek. What a handsome boy, she was thinking, so lifelike, he feels real and he's so well proportioned. Then she saw the syringe and without more thought, she pulled it from his arm. The prince stirred, the anthropologist jumped back startled. The prince stretched, opened his eyes, yawned and blinked. He stood up unsteadily and stumbled. The anthropologist stepped forward and took his arm and the prince exclaimed, 'Who are you?'

There was a great deal of explaining to do on both sides and when they left the room they found that the king and queen, all the guests, courtiers and the servants had woken up and were milling around in a confusion. Then the second good fairy jumped up onto the king's throne and clapped his hands for silence. 'You've all been asleep for years and years, the prince fell into a coma, as was predicted on the day of his christening, but the right woman has turned up and all is well.'

The good fairy looked at the anthropologist and said, 'You're a good few years older than him, but you're still very young and you've saved him, so I think that now the two of you are going to live happily ever after.'

'Rubbish, I'm going to go back to my university to write a report on all of this and it could well make me famous. But in the meantime, since I rescued the prince and since he's such a handsome creature, I'm more than ready to make him happy for a day or two.' And she led the willing prince to his bedroom where she showed him that sex was a great deal nicer than addictive drugs, which as the first good fairy said to the second good fairy, 'is a more suitable ending to a modern fairy story than happily ever after'.

My Name is Erica

My name is Erica; I'm fourteen years old. The worst thing I've done so far in my life is to make love to my brother-in-law and now my sister won't talk to me. She's in the garden, lying curled up on a rug on the lawn and ignoring her two children. The baby is grizzling and the toddler is pulling heads off our mum's few flowers. I don't see it as my business to stop him, although Ma won't be pleased when she comes back from town. She's gone shopping for food, or so she says, having my sister and her family staying with us means she has to do a lot of extra housework, and that she hates.

They arrived last week. My sister, Alison, telephoned on Saturday afternoon and I answered.

'Is Ma in?' she said.

'Nope, just me, you'll have to put up with me.'

I could hear her sighing. 'When's she back?'

'Dunno. She's gone to have lunch with a new boyfriend. Don't suppose they'll be home for ages.' I blew a great big bubble with my chewing gum and it burst.

'You crying?' I asked Alison.

'No,' she said, but there were tears in her answer.

'Why you phoning? You after something?'

'We want to come and stay, we want to come this afternoon.'

'Why? Been thrown out of the commune?' There was silence, so I knew I'd got it right.

My sister is a hippie and so's her husband, Steve. She left home when she was sixteen and got pregnant almost straight away. She came with Steve to tell us, but she didn't really need to, you could see her tummy was round even under the floaty clothes she wears. Our mum couldn't really say very much, given the kind of life she leads; I've lost count of the number of her men friends me and Alison have had to put up with. She looked at Alison and lit another cigarette and sighed.

'What do you want me to say, congratulations? I don't know that I feel old enough to be a grandmother.' That was two years ago, 1970, and Ma was not yet forty and looked lots younger. Men really fancied her, still do. I could see Steve looking at her in that way and looking puzzled at the same time, I don't think he expected to find his future ma-in-law so attractive. As for him, I thought he was a real dish, tall and muscular with enormous blue eyes but dark hair. He's got such a pretty face it's a good thing his body is so masculine, else you might think he was a girl.

'We're going to get married, aren't we Steve?' He didn't answer; he was the silent type.

'Steve!' Alison shook his shoulder.

'Oh, yeah.' He nodded. He didn't look that enthusiastic,

nor did he at the wedding, nor when they brought their first baby Frith to stay with us, nor when they came to tell us another one was on the way. Felix was born just a year and a day after his brother. Ma and I went to see them all and when we arrived, Steve was sitting in the garden, leaning against the wall of the house, smoking dope. He nodded to us as we came through the gate, but didn't get up. He watched us as we walked up the path and as he did, he started to smile and his eyes turned flirty.

'Want a toke?' he asked, waving the joint at us.

'No,' said my mum. She smokes cigarettes and drinks a lot, and although she knows about drugs, she's scared of them. She's not quite the right generation, I suppose, and when I squatted down and took the joint, she smacked the back of my head.

'You're not old enough for that.' I ignored her and inhaled deeply.

'S'not the first time, Ma,' I said and Steve laughed.

We didn't stay long, Alison was tired and there seemed to be some sort of row going on between the commune members. While we were inside one of the men came home and we could hear him shouting at Steve.

'Hey, man, what ya doing? You supposed to be mending the fucking fence.'

'Oh piss off, I'll do it when I'm good and ready, you're not my boss and life is for living, not working.' I think it was the longest sentence I'd ever heard Steve use, but he still sounded relaxed, not angry at all. One of the women put her head out of the window and joined in.

'Come on Steve, we've all got our chores to do.'

'Leave him alone, he's tired, the baby kept us awake last night,' said Alison and the woman turned and stared at her, shaking her head.

'Oh yeah? He was up till late getting stoned, wasn't the baby keeping him awake.'

And now they've been thrown out and come to live with our mum and me. Ma owns the house, our dad signed it over to her after they split up and for a time it was full of lodgers. But when I started school, she went back to work and gradually the lodgers left. Just as well, as there are only three bedrooms. The kids are in with Alison and Steve.

They arrived that Saturday before Ma had come home, in their old van that Steve had started to paint pink and green and psychedelic. He's only done part of one side and the rest is boring brown. Alison was upset and Steve was silent, except when he was telling Frith to shut up; Frith was whinging.

'How long you planning on staying?' I asked.

'Don't know, we need time to decide what to do next, don't we Steve?'

'Ma might not be too keen, there's this new man around, and in any case there's not much room.'

'I'm her daughter; she won't throw me out. These are her grandchildren.'

'You should know, Alison, she's not the motherly type and being a grandmother cramps her style a bit.'

Steve was rolling up. I turned to him.

'And she's not that keen on joints, you'd better be careful.'

Steve laughed. 'I'll see if I can't get her using the stuff.' He carried on rolling and laughing and as he lit up he winked at me, a very slow, very deliberate wink and I felt sort of liquidy inside and I knew I was going to sleep with him and the sooner, the better.

Alison had put the boys down for the night before Ma came home. I'd helped her make up the bed and the cot in the spare room, feed Frith and bath him and I'd even read him a story, not that he understood it, but I think he liked the sound of my voice reading. I don't know what I feel about my nephews, I don't think I love them, I don't feel old enough to be an aunt. They almost seem like large troublesome dolls that Alison is playing with. And it's hard to think of Alison as a mother, she tries hard to look after the boys properly, too hard, perhaps. But that's the way she is, not just with the kids but with everything.

We were sitting in the garden, Steve was drinking beer, and Alison was sewing a button onto one of Frith's shirts, when we heard our mum come in. The new man was with her and they both came into the garden, Ma looking irritated and the man pushy and possessive.

'What you two doing here?'

'We've had to leave the commune, we've come to stay for a bit.' Alison was biting her lip and squeezing the shirt between her hands.

'You might have asked first.'

'I phoned, you weren't here. We had to leave quickly.' Alison blushed and looked at Steve, but he said nothing.

Neither did Ma; she just shrugged her shoulders and pouted.

'Are you going to introduce me?' the new man asked.

'Yes, yes, sorry, my elder daughter, Alison and her husband, Steve. Erica you've met. This is Pete.' She paused. 'Well, Pete, since my family has unexpectedly arrived I'll be spending the evening with them. Sorry, but... another time. I'll see you to your car.' Pete patted her bum in a proprietorial way I didn't like, and I knew she didn't either. The new man was swiftly becoming ex-man. After he'd gone Ma opened some wine and I left, I had a date. When I came home, Alison was in bed and Ma and Steve were pissed.

That was last Saturday and it's Saturday again today. It's been a pretty awful week on the whole, the second of my summer holidays. The only bits that have been any good was being in bed with Steve, but since Alison found us at it that's probably over now. In any case, although I don't regret it, it really was a wicked thing to do. And I suspect Alison's going to tell Ma. Don't know what she'll have to say about it.

Ma got up late last Sunday and said, 'Well you're all in luck, I've decided to cook you a proper roast lunch.' Ma's a good cook when she wants to be and there was a chicken in the fridge that had originally been planned for the evening before. Lunch was great, and we had wine, but my mum was sharp with Frith, who sat in his highchair, whining and turning his head away from whatever Alison gave him to eat. After we'd cleared away and washed up, Ma indicated that it would be nice if the children could be removed from the house to give her a break, and so Alison and I took them to the local park.

'Try and stay out till tea time,' Ma yelled from the door as we left the house.

'You'd think she'd be more interested in her grandchildren,' Alison moaned. I shrugged.

'It's the good life she likes, Alison, remember when we were little, she loved us, but she wasn't very interested in being a mother or a housewife.'

'It was OK, we weren't neglected. She stayed at home and looked after us.'

'Yeah, but she still preferred going out, remember how sparkly she used to get when she was dressing up for a date.'

When we came home, our mum and Steve were lazing in the garden. They'd opened another bottle of wine and were smoking, Steve a joint, Ma a cigarette.

None of us helped Alison to feed the children and put them to bed. We just sat around in the garden and she came and joined us looking cross and tired. When Ma went in and found the bathroom in a shambles she opened the window and shouted into the garden.

'For God's sake Alison, clean up after yourself, please. There's not enough room in the house for all of us and it's far worse when it's untidy.' And that went on all week, the kids creating disorder, Steve too lazy to do anything about it, Alison too tired and busy to care and Ma getting angry at her.

Monday Ma went to work and I went to meet some friends at the swimming pool, I came home and helped Alison prepare some lunch. She was really frazzled, she kept sighing and every now and then she'd shout at Steve or Frith.

'Steve, can't you clear up the toys in the living room? Ma'll go potty if they're still there when she comes home… Stop whining, Frith and let go of my legs.' Frith spent most of his time clinging on to Alison with his thumb in his mouth. When she was really fed up she'd pick him up and dump him on Steve's knees. The two would communicate in a silent sort of way for a minute or two, and then Frith would climb down and either go in search of his mum or start playing with things he wasn't supposed to touch.

She moaned at me, 'You're so lucky, Erica, look at my life compared to yours.' I didn't want to point out that she'd chosen to run off and had stupidly got pregnant twice before she was eighteen. I wasn't intending to do any such thing, I'd never make love without taking precautions.

After lunch I told her I'd wash and tidy up if she'd take the children out to the park, and so she did. And I went and sat in the garden with Steve. I shared his joint, leant on his knees, and made sure that he could see how sexy my body was.

It wasn't long before he kissed me and then we went upstairs to my room. But before we'd taken all our clothes off he said, 'Hey, you're rather young, I do'n wanna be the first.'

'You're not,' I told him. I discovered sex a few months ago and I'd already had two lovers, but none as exciting as Steve. I'd also got myself fixed up with contraception, which is difficult when you're my age, but if you're resourceful, as I am, you can find a way. Steve was impatient when I stopped him so that I could put in my Dutch cap, but afterwards it was wonderful. He didn't say much, but I loved caressing his body and the way he kissed and touched me.

I got him out of my bed before Alison came home and did a bit of cleaning. Ma was in a bad mood when she came home because the place was seriously untidy and told us all to clear up while she went to get a takeaway. And the week slid by like that: mess and bad temper, but whenever we found ourselves alone Steve and I made love. Mostly it was during the day when Alison went out with the kids, but we had one evening when Ma took Alison to the cinema to stop her complaining about how she never went out. We were always careful to be dressed and apart by the time Alison was due home, until this morning, but that wasn't our fault, she'd changed her mind and come home almost as soon as she'd left.

Ma went off into town early, she said she had a lot to do and wouldn't be back for lunch. Alison didn't want to take the kids out, but Steve said, 'If you don't take them, they'll mess the place up and we'll have to tidy up.'

'I'll have to tidy up, you mean,' Alison said.

'Whatever, just get the kids out of the house, will ya?'

Alison looked at him as she does these days, as if she wondered who he was and why she was bothering with him. But she took the kids off to the park and Steve and I went straight up to my room. Each time we made love it was better than the last and I was sitting on Steve and moaning when my bedroom door flung open and there was Alison. She stood there, her face red and runny-looking, her mouth open. It was then that I realised just how bad we were being.

'You bitch,' she said finally, her voice high with disbelief. Steve said nothing and then Felix started wailing and Alison turned and left the room. I got up and dressed, while Steve just lay there.

'You'd better get up, what you going to do, what you going to say?'

He shrugged.

'Well, Steve, you've got to do something!'

'She'll get over it.'

'What about you and me?'

'S'pose we'd better stop, or be more careful.'

Finally he got up. 'Going out for a bit,' he said. Escaping more like, I thought, but I said nothing, I went into the garden and there was Alison, crying on the rug.

'I'm sorry,' I said.

'Don't be silly, it's not something you can be sorry for, it's something you should never have done, I dunno what's worse, him betraying me, you betraying me, or you being still a child. I've got to tell Ma, what if you get pregnant?' Her face was swollen and angry and I did feel sorry for her, not so much for what I've done as for what she's done to her life. Me, I'm not going to be like her: no way.

'Don't worry, I won't get pregnant.'

'Just go away, leave me alone, I never want to see you again, I never want to speak to you again,' she said.

And she's been curled up on that rug now for nearly an hour and though I've offered to make her tea or a sandwich, she won't talk.

Our mum's just come home. 'For God's sake, what's she doing, letting the kids loose in my garden,' she's saying, going into the garden and I follow. She picks up the grizzling baby and pulls Frith out of the flowerbed; he's got soil all over his mouth, she stands and looks at the mound on the rug.

'Alison, get up now, the kids need you.'

Alison unrolls and starts to cry. She sits up and looks up at our mum and she says, a sob between each word and her voice as whiny as her son's, 'It's Erica, Ma, she's a bitch and a pig and… I found her this morning, in bed with Steve, making love.'

Ma's turning to look at me, her eyes wide open and her nostrils slightly flared.

'You, too,' she's saying.

Meeting Dad

Mum put the phone down and turned to them, her mouth a straight hard line.

'That,' she said, giving a big sigh, 'was your Nelson grandma.'

Millie looked at Daisy, reaching out to hold her hand. Daisy would start crying if Mum went on sounding cross, Millie knew, and because she was older she also knew that her job was to protect her little sister. That and asking the right questions.

'Why did she phone?' Millie asked.

Mum let out a strange puffy noise, marched across the room and opened the fridge. 'I need a drink.' She took out a big bottle, unscrewed the top, poured some of the yellowy liquid into a glass and took a big swig.

'We've to go to Nelson for the weekend. It's Fathers' Day, your grandma says. He's out and wants to see you.'

Mum sat in the big armchair that was losing its stuffing and crossed her legs. 'It's at times like this I wish I still smoked,' she said.

'Why are we going to Nelson?' Millie asked.

'For you to meet your good-for-nothing father again,' Mum said. She finished her glass, stood up and refilled it.

A strange thrill filled Millie's body. She couldn't tell if it was a nice or nasty feeling but it had to do with the idea of seeing her father. She wasn't sure if she could remember him. There were shadowy memories of a big man with dark hair throwing her into the air to make her laugh and others of Mum and the man arguing, waking her and Daisy up, shouting in the middle of the night. Once she'd walked into the hall from their bedroom and there had been two policemen talking to the man. Mum had been crying. Millie wasn't sure if that was a dream or something that had really happened.

'She's bought the plane tickets, the interfering old bag. Booked me a motel room. You two are to stay with her for the night,' Mum said.

Daisy started to cry. 'Don't want to stay with a bag,' she wailed and Mum started to laugh.

In bed that night Daisy whispered, 'I didn't know we had a dad.'

Millie explained that everyone has a dad, even if you didn't live with him. Daisy asked why they hadn't seen him before. Millie tried to think of a good answer but finally all she could say was, 'He's been away. Now he's come back.'

Although Mum was in a bad mood, it was fun flying to Nelson. The plane was so small that Mum had a seat on her own on one side of the aisle and Millie and Daisy sat together on the other side. Mum stared out of the window for most of the journey even though she'd bought a magazine that was sitting on her lap.

'There's your grandma,' Mum said after they'd landed and were in the airport. A thin woman was walking towards them, smiling. She had long black hair and wore shoes with high heels.

'Hello,' she said. Her voice sounded like gravel being walked on. 'How you two have grown, I hardly recognised you.'

Daisy frowned. 'You don't look like a real grandma,' she said, peering up.

Mum told Daisy not to be rude, shaking her head. Millie thought it was only pretend cross. She took Daisy's hand and followed Mum and Grandma into the car park.

'Maybe she's a witch,' Daisy whispered to Millie as they stood waiting for the grandma woman to unlock the car.

'I think I seen her before, when you were just a baby,' Millie whispered back.

'Don't suppose you want to come and meet Brad?' the grandma asked Mum when they were in the car.

'No way,' Mum said. She was sitting hunched up as if she didn't want to be there. Millie helped Daisy open the bag of chips the grandma had given her, then she opened her own. They were her favourites, barbecued bacon.

'And no need to think you can bribe the kids to liking you with junk food,' Mum said.

The grandma laughed. 'S'pose they're used to gourmet cooking, are they?'

Mum didn't answer, just hunched herself up even more.

They dropped Mum at a motel. She peered into the back of the car, telling them that she'd see them tomorrow and to be good girls. Then she walked away. Daisy started to whimper.

'Don't cry, chick,' the grandma said. 'I'm used to kids. We'll go and fetch your dad. He's longing to see you and then we'll get burgers for lunch.'

Millie took hold of Daisy's hand as they walked behind the grandma into her house. She pushed open the door and called, 'Brad. We're home.'

Millie felt Daisy's fingers clinging onto hers and knew that her little sister was frightened. 'Don't be scared,' she whispered. 'He's only a dad. Not a monster.'

They stood in the hallway, just inside the door, very close to each other. A man came through a door and stood looking at them. It couldn't be their dad because he wasn't as big as Millie remembered. He had his arms folded and his hair was cut so short it was as if it was painted on.

'Well,' he said after a while. He shook his head. 'My little girls. You were tiny things the last time I saw you.'

'Is that our dad?' Daisy whispered and the man laughed.

'Course I am.' He knelt down so that his head was at the same level as Daisy's. 'Do I get a kiss?' he asked.

'No,' Daisy said. Millie felt her pressing closer to her than ever; she was trembling.

'Maybe later,' Millie said, wanting to be polite. 'When we've got to know you better.'

'Fair enough,' the dad said and stood up.

In the hamburger place, Grandma let them choose what they wanted. And they were allowed to have milkshakes, too. Millie found it hard to eat even though she thought she was hungry. Grandma and Dad chatted to each other but she couldn't think of anything to say. She wondered what little girls were supposed to talk to their dads about. When she went to her friends' houses, if there were dads around they usually didn't talk but sat watching telly or reading papers. Sometimes they drank beer. Once Millie had taken a sip from a beer can and found it tasted disgusting. She asked Dad if he liked beer.

'Course I do,' Dad said. 'Do you?'

'No.' Millie shook her head.

'Did you once live with us?' Daisy asked. She had finished all her food and no longer seemed to be scared.

'Yeah. Once.'

'Why don't you any longer?'

'Well.' He was stroking his chin.

'Tell them straight, Brad. Sylvie threw you out,' Grandma said in her gravelly voice.

'Wasn't quite like that, Ma,' Dad said.

'They don't want to know the ins and outs. They're just kids.'

She would like to know the 'ins and outs' whatever they were, Millie thought. Grown-ups were strange the way they tried to hide things but expected children to tell the truth.

'Did you go in and out?' Daisy asked.

Dad laughed. 'That's one way of putting it, yes. I was in and now I'm out. Who'd like to go to the park?'

'Me!' Daisy called. Millie felt cross with her little sister. She seemed to be happy to accept this man as their dad while she, Millie, who was the one who almost remembered him, wasn't yet sure. She kicked the table leg and pushed away the remains of her food. No one seemed to notice. If Mum had been there, she'd have told her to behave.

In the park, Dad helped them on the swings while Grandma sat on a bench and used her cellphone. Then he watched them on the climbing frame.

'Look at me,' Daisy called as she hung upside down and then again when she stood on the very top.

They had jelly and ice cream for tea and Daisy asked Dad if he was going to read them a bedtime story. He asked if that was what their mum did.

'When she's in a good mood,' Daisy explained.

'Which she normally is,' Millie added, not wanting to give the wrong impression.

'I'll have to tell you a story out of my head,' Dad said. 'We don't have any kids' books.'

As they lay in bed, he told them a story about a man who had two daughters that he loved. But the ruler of the country where they lived came to see the man and said that he needed his help in fighting cruel enemies so the man had to leave his daughters for years and years while he went around making sure all the enemies were killed. When he came back, the daughters had forgotten that the man was their father. The man said that if they kissed him they would remember who he was, so first the little girl and then the big girl did just that and they all lived happily ever after.

'Is that what you've been doing?' Daisy asked.

'Something like that,' Dad said.

'If I kiss you will I remember you?' she asked.

'Let's try,' Dad said and Daisy sat up, put her arms around him and kissed him. 'Well?' Dad asked.

'I think I do. I think you must be my dad,' Daisy said, speaking quietly, a little shy.

'Well Millie?' Dad asked. Millie shook her head. She was not ready yet.

'Do you like him?' Daisy asked Millie when the light was switched off, the door closed and they were alone.

'Don't know,' Millie said. She yawned and turned over. Soon she would be asleep.

The next day Grandma said she would make a roast lunch and while she was cooking, Dad took Millie and Daisy to the beach even though it wasn't summer. Daisy tried to turn a cartwheel and Millie showed Dad how to do it properly.

As they were going back to Grandma's Dad said to Millie, 'I didn't want to leave you, I didn't choose it. Will you stop being angry and forgive me for going?'

Millie did feel angry but she wasn't sure why. Probably it was because he was trying to come back rather than because he had left, she thought. So she didn't reply.

After lunch, Grandma took out an envelope. 'I've some photos,' she said, spilling them out onto the table. There weren't many. But the one Millie liked best was of Dad holding her high in the air when she was just a tiny girl. They were staring at each other, smiling and smiling.

It was time to pick Mum up and go to the airport. Dad asked would they come and see him again. He sounded as if he might cry but he couldn't, because men can't cry.

Millie turned to Daisy and asked, 'Would you like to?'

Daisy nodded. 'I think it's quite nice to have a dad, really.'

'Or I could come down to you,' Dad said.

'Yes,' Millie said. 'We'd like that.'

He knelt, pulling both girls close to him. Millie felt his rough cheek rubbing hers and she relaxed against him. Daisy was right. It probably would be quite nice to have a dad. Millie pulled away before leaning in to kiss him.

This is not Miranda's Story

Miranda moved towards me with her new baby, carrying it like a child would carry a broken doll. And I knew then that what Tim had been trying to tell me was true. She was staring straight ahead and her face was impassive. It always had been. She had a square, jutting jaw; full, firm lips; smooth flawless skin. As she came closer, along the pavement, I realised that I had never seen her smile. Not once in all the time I had known her. She stopped and stared at me with eyes that held no expression.

Reaching out to the baby, I pulled him to me, Miranda's hand still grasped tightly round his wrist. She looked at me as if I were a stranger. She was calm, almost serene. I brought the baby closer to me, cradling him in my arms as her grip slowly released. She turned and went back the way she'd come. I stood watching, expecting her to go up her drive and into her house, where I imagined that Tim and Hayden, her first child, were waiting for her, but she carried on, down the street, walking as if she had purpose.

Tim brought Miranda back from Sydney with him. That's not quite true. He visited Sydney a number of times and eventually told us that he was to marry a woman he had met there.

'Tomorrow I'm fetching her from the airport. She is quite lovely,' he said in his low, unemotional voice.

'Just the sort of voice an accountant would have,' was how my husband, Gary, once described it. Ex-husband now, though we were still married at the time Tim found Miranda.

Tim's car went slowly past our house and turned into his drive. There was a woman sitting next to him, quite still. She had long brown hair. The fiancée, I thought. I reached for a paper towel and dried my eyes. I had been crying as I stared out of the kitchen window, wondering if there was anything I could do to make Gary want to stay. He had fallen out of love with me. That was not how he expressed it; it was what I said to myself when I was alone, making myself feel the pain of what was happening to Gary and me. I said it to goad myself into despair, hoping that if I cried enough the misery would drain away and I could be normal again. The problem was that Gary could not quite make up his mind. Sometimes he would come and put his arms round me, hold me and rock me, his face pressed against mine so that I could feel the damp roughness of his skin, and his particular smell – slightly acrid, slightly sweet – would envelope me.

So when I first met Miranda my senses were heightened by the uncertainty of my life. I was fragile and emotional. She was tall, and still and strong – seemed strong, seemed stable. We met her at a party that Tim held a few weekends after she'd arrived. Just the neighbours; early evening; a little strained. There was beer and wine (with a cheap over-fruity flavour; I only had a few sips before putting my glass down), some peanuts in a bowl and chips, as if forgotten, still in their packets on the kitchen bench. The place hadn't changed since Miranda had moved in. There were no flowers, few pictures on the wall, no ornaments or cushions, rugs or throws. She had added no woman's touch to the bland beige of Tim's furnishings. And she never did.

Miranda stood in the same place for the hour that we were there. She held a tumbler of orange juice between both hands and spoke to everyone as they came up to her. She was wearing a grey soft cotton skirt that fell to her ankles, a plain white sleeveless blouse, no make-up, no jewellery. I looked down at her feet at one point and was taken by her chunky brown sandals and wide toes with neatly trimmed unpainted nails. She was, I thought, the perfect woman for Tim, with her serious unadorned beauty.

'Why don't you dress more like her?' Gary said when we came home. He looked me up and down. I was wearing yellow culottes with a pink stripe, a thin summer jacket to match over a T-shirt in the same yellow with pink spots and, on my feet, pink suede boots. He went to the fridge to find another beer and I stood not wanting to move for fear that a scream would escape my mouth and scare the neighbours. Once, when we were students, Gary had liked my flamboyant style. He never said but I could tell from how he used to look at me, with his face on one side, his eyes narrowed and a little smile just touching his lips.

I'm trying to explain Miranda. The problem is that I can't think of how she was then without remembering how I was, too. We couldn't become friends. She wasn't interested in what was happening to me. And that was the only thing I could cope with in those months when she and Tim were first married and Gary and I were peeling apart. So I saw her from time to time and saw how Tim looked at her, standing a little to one side of her, smiling, proud. I think he wondered how he, boring and stolid, could have persuaded her to come to this little New Zealand town and live with him.

Well.

Gary moved out. We tried counselling but he just sat, looking shifty in the cheap armchair with its faux wood arms and thin brown upholstery. Sometimes one of his feet would tap on the worn linoleum. When we walked to the car afterwards, he'd sigh out a big breath of air as if he'd been holding it in for the forty minutes of the session. So he left and I moved two lodgers in and paid him for his share of the house. I saw him a few months later in a bar with a blonde woman. She was wearing satin shorts and a tight gold-spangled top.

During this time, Miranda settled in. Or so I assume. I saw her sometimes walking up the street with a big leather satchel over her shoulder. She didn't drive. She didn't find a job either. Sometimes we spoke, at neighbourhood gatherings, occasionally when I was in my front garden and she came striding home. She told me she was doing research but didn't specify what it was about. When I asked her what her speciality was she looked at me and blinked as if the question were odd.

170

I used to meet her in the local library. Once I stood next to her at the checkout desk. She was filling her satchel with books. They were an eclectic mix, the ones I saw, non-fiction: one on New Zealand birds, another on the sinking of the Titanic, a third on the philosophy of Immanuel Kant.

'How're you doing?' I asked.

'I'm getting there,' she said. She paused. She added, 'The categorical imperative. I think I've found it.'

'Right,' I said and nodded, not understanding.

It was even before her first pregnancy that Tim started to have concerns. I didn't pay them much heed at the time. We were sitting next to each other at a barbecue in someone's garden and he was, as usual, watching Miranda. She was perched on the children's swing near the back fence, moving herself almost imperceptibly to and fro. Tim sighed.

'What's the matter?' I asked, turning to look at him. He moved his face, just a little, so I could see that behind his glasses his eyes were an astonishing green – I'd not noticed that before – and that they were flecked with worry.

'Nothing... nothing... really...' he said and when he stopped I knew he had more to say. Eventually, 'D'you think she's all right?' he asked.

'Miranda?'

'Yes. D'you think maybe she's missing Sydney?'

'Have you asked her?'

'No. It's... did you know she has no family? Both her parents are dead and her brother went overseas and disappeared.'

'I didn't know,' I said. I looked at Miranda on her own, swaying slightly back and forth, and I thought that maybe she was not the serious person she appeared to be, but someone who was in mourning. 'Long ago?' I asked.

Tim shrugged. 'Not sure. You see… I'm not an asking sort of person.'

'And she's not a telling sort?' I suggested.

'She's not,' he said. But he smiled. Something about Miranda was making him smile.

'But you're happy together and that's what counts,' I said. Or rather asked. Tim nodded, though he looked uncertain, and I stood up and moved away. I wanted more cheerful company. That night I sat on my porch – it was one of those late summer balmy evenings – and thought about Tim's surprising green eyes.

There were some difficulties during the pregnancy, not physical ones, just Miranda not being at home when Tim came back from work and he, later, at ten or eleven at night, knocking on neighbours' doors and asking if anyone had seen her. It happened a few times.

'She's got herself a lover,' the widow who lived next to me said one Saturday morning. She'd been pottering about in her vegetable garden and I'd been hanging out my washing thinking about another weekend evening with nowhere to go and no one to go with. I'd finished pegging the last sheet as she stood up and we started talking, she leaning on the dividing wall with a trowel in her hand, her face lit by a gleeful interest in local scandal.

I moved closer to her and asked, 'Are you sure? She's going to have a baby in a few months.'

'Why else...' She paused. 'Why else would she be off in the evenings? Maybe the baby's not Tim's.' She had lowered her voice and raised her eyebrows.

'No,' I said. 'She's too serious for that.'

'It's the quiet ones you have to watch,' she said. 'You, for example, no one would suspect you of shenanigans. You are what you seem.'

'Oh,' I said, not knowing what she meant.

She laughed. 'That's a compliment, dear,' she said.

When a few evenings later Tim knocked at my door asking if I'd seen Miranda, I invited him in. I offered him a hot drink and he sat in my kitchen and drank camomile tea. I'd told him it was relaxing.

'Where was she the last times she was missing?' I asked him. He said nothing, shook his head.

'Well?' I insisted.

'I don't know. She never said.'

'But she came home,' I said.

'Yes. Once, not till two in the morning. What should I do?' he asked. As if I had an answer. 'I better go,' he said. 'I shouldn't have stopped. I just...'

'Needed to be with someone for a while?' I knew, I think, how he felt.

I touched his arm as he was leaving, a little gesture of comfort and he turned back to look at me and smiled. He had a wonderful smile.

Once the baby was born – a boy called Hayden – I often saw Miranda out in the street early in the mornings even before I went to work, pushing the pram. It was big and old-fashioned, black and stately and it made me think of Miranda as the boy's nursemaid rather than his mother. I half expected her to start wearing a uniform; I imagined her in a crisp blue print dress, white starched apron with a little matching cap and a severe navy coat with epaulettes and brass buttons. It was about that time that Tim started to work from home. He turned the front living room into an office and put up a small sign. I asked him about it one Saturday when he was out with the baby. Pushing him in a buggy, not the pram that Miranda used.

'Started your own business, I see, Tim. Hope it's working out.'

'Yes. Yes. I had to. She… I had enough clients and Miranda… I need to be there for Hayden,' he said. He looked sad. Or maybe harassed. I felt he wanted to say more and I waited for it. But he just cleared his throat.

I said, 'Pop in for a cup of tea later if you want to.' And I went back into the house.

He rang the bell about an hour after that and I let him and the baby in. I hadn't expected that he'd come but was glad he had. I was beginning to like him. I think it was because he was tentative and seemed vulnerable but was also solid. I imagined depending on him. I imagined him coming home and me saying, 'Oh, I think we have a problem with the guttering,' and him going to the garage for the ladder, propping it carefully against the wall, slowly mounting, turning round when he reached the top and saying to me, 'You're right. It needs cleaning, I'll start straightaway.' I flushed as I thought this: it seemed so intimate.

'Gary would never do anything about the house,' I said as I turned to fill the jug with water. The words came out unexpectedly and I wondered what Tim would make of them. With the back of my hand, I touched my cheeks, first one then the other. They felt hot. 'I've some biscuits somewhere,' I said, still not facing Tim. I found the packet behind some tins in the cupboard, chocolate fingers, and put them on a plate. Tim was fussing with the baby, re-settling him into the buggy. When he stood up, he smiled at me and sat at the table to drink his tea.

That afternoon Tim told me that he had arranged for him and Miranda to see a psychiatrist, that he wasn't sure if Miranda was coping well with Hayden.

'She loves him. Of course. But…'

'He looks fine to me,' I told him. Not that I had any experience. He was six months old now and stared at me, with his big brown eyes: solemn like his mother's.

'She lets him cry. She won't go to him,' Tim was saying. He took one of the biscuits and bit into it. 'She carries him about sometimes, as if he… wasn't real. I have to take him from her…'

I understood that he was worried and wished there were something I could do; something I could say. 'She must miss not having a family,' I offered.

Tim nodded. He still looked uncertain. 'Maybe that's it. And we'll see what the shrink thinks,' he said. He put down the biscuit, half-eaten. He left soon after and I walked from room to room in my little house, even my lodgers' rooms, knocking first, of course. I wished that there were somewhere I wanted to go.

It became a habit, Tim coming to see me for a short time on Saturday afternoons. Once I even made a cake. But Tim only took a small slice of that and the lodgers finished it the next day, eating it instead of lunch.

Miranda was now seeing the psychiatrist on her own, once a fortnight and she was still working at her research. She went to the library nearly every morning. Once when Hayden was ill she still insisted that she needed to go. She became quite frantic when Tim asked her to stay at home with the baby. All this he told me, in snippets, as he drank his tea.

'What is her research?' I asked. Just once.

'She… doesn't like to talk about it,' Tim said. He looked uneasy and left soon after.

'Do you think Miranda is normal?' he asked me a few months later when Hayden was coming up to his first birthday. He now went to a day nursery. Tim took him in the mornings and fetched him again late in the afternoon.

'What does her shrink say?' I asked.

He shrugged. 'We don't discuss that…' He looked at me, blinking, needing a response.

So, 'Why do you think Miranda's not normal?' I gave him.

'You're right,' he said. 'How would I know what a

normal woman is like.' He gave a little laugh. It seemed to me – looking at him and thinking how he had pretty lips, which would be good to kiss – that he gave out little hints of unhappiness and then couldn't go any further. I thought of them as puffs of steam pushing out of his mouth that released some of the pressure building up inside him. Once they were spoken they drifted about like little clouds and took a long time to disappear.

The day he told me that Miranda was pregnant again he sat for a long time with his head in his hands, looking down at the table, every now and then moving his fingers, massaging the sorrowful thoughts that were filling his head.

'She can't cope with one. How are we going to manage two?' He had taken off his glasses and looked up at me with his naked eyes. I wanted to bend down and kiss the pain out of them. I didn't. 'And she is ill. Mentally,' he said, putting his glasses back on and reaching for his teacup. As Tim was talking, Hayden, sitting on the floor, had been staring at his father.

'No,' I said. I meant it. In spite of her fortnightly sessions with a psychiatrist, there was nothing mad about Miranda, I was sure. She didn't shriek and yell and talk about seeing things that weren't there.

'No?' Tim asked.

'She's just serious,' I said. 'She's involved in her research.'

'She's obsessed. And I don't know if the research is… real.'

'Don't worry.' I wanted him to smile at me. And truly, then, I didn't think there was anything the matter with Miranda.

Later that day the bell rang and I thought it was Tim coming back. I don't know why I should have imagined that, but it made me sit up in anticipation. I heard one of my lodgers padding to the front door, the creak as it opened and then the murmur of conversation.

The lodger called, 'You've a visitor.'

I went into the hall and there was Gary looking as if he knew I'd be pleased to see him.

'What happened to the woman in the gold-spangled top?' I snapped.

'What?' He frowned.

'Oh,' I said. 'Well,' I said. 'Why are you here?'

'To see you,' he said.

'But why?'

'I thought... maybe we could go out. Talk. See where we're at. You know.'

I shook my head. 'You think we could try and get our relationship back?' I asked. I looked at him, tall, good-looking, hair expensively cut, tiny gold ring in one ear, quirky and stylish clothes. When we were first together other women would stare at him admiringly. I used to enjoy those stares and the little possessive smile I'd send back.

He was looking at me, head on one side, eyes slightly narrowed, a slight curl to his lips. He wanted to touch me. I was his, he was thinking; his, even after all this time apart.

'No,' I said and he opened his mouth to try and persuade me otherwise. After I'd made him go, I sat in my living room and thought about Tim. Night came and I went to bed. I'd not done anything that evening, not even eaten a meal or had a cup of tea.

I saw Miranda in the library some weeks later. I stood and watched as she took books off the shelves, opened them, turned a few pages, read for a bit, then put them back. After a while she selected one and moved away up the aisle. She had a graceful walk, I thought, and was calm and controlled. Not in the least mad as Tim had feared. I wasn't sure what I felt about that.

Next day I saw her in the early morning. I was in the kitchen drinking tea and staring out on the street as I waited for my toast to brown. She came out of the entrance to their drive pushing the big black pram. I moved closer to the window and peered out. I saw that Hayden was in the pram, sitting up, not smiling. He was a placid little boy, about eighteen months old at the time. Miranda was walking quickly away from the house and then Tim came running out. He reached her and touched her arm. She stopped and I could see he was talking to her. She shook her head and started to push the pram again, quickly. Tim followed her. He was bare foot, I noticed. She turned and said something to him and then carried on, walking fast. He stood watching her and then he shook his head and started after her. He caught her up, took Hayden out of the pram and headed back home. Miranda didn't move for a little while. She was holding onto the handle of the pram with both hands, her head a little bowed and then she shook it and continued down the road, pushing the pram, staring straight ahead, as was her wont.

Tim told me about it the next Saturday when I mentioned what I'd seen.

'I think she is mad,' he said.

'What did she say to you when you tried to stop her?' I asked.

'She said she was taking Hayden for a walk.' He paused. 'She actually said, "I am taking my son out for fresh air. I'm concerned about the cobwebs in his head." Now that's odd. It is, isn't it?'

'She just has… a particular way of speaking,' I said.

'But she carried on, even after I'd taken Hayden.' Tim pushed his fist down to emphasise the strangeness of the action he was describing. He did it again. Another man, I thought, would have thumped the table. I wanted to stroke his face and comfort him. I wanted to kiss him and hold him. I wanted to ease the pain out of him. My thoughts were with Tim and not Miranda as I sat next to him and took his hand, trying to unclench his fingers. I reached up and touched his hair with my other hand, stroked it.

He looked at me as if seeing me for the first time. 'Don't,' he said. He moved his chair back, and his head and hands away from me. 'Miranda is my wife and I am deeply concerned about her,' he said. His voice was gentle and accusing at the same time.

'I just…' I could not find the words to try and excuse my gestures. I could not tell him that they stemmed from love. The problem was that they did; of that I was almost sure.

'It's OK,' he said. 'It's OK.' After he'd left, I sat on in the kitchen and wondered what that meant.

Tim didn't come to see me for several Saturdays after that. I didn't see Miranda, either. My widowed neighbour told me that they'd gone away for a few weeks.

'Does she still have that lover?' I asked her.

'Oh that,' she said. 'It was just rumour. Don't think there was any truth in it. Though the little boy… doesn't look like Tim at all, does he? He's an odd child, too. Far too quiet, I'd say. He'll explode later and then there'll be trouble.' She sounded satisfied at the idea and I tried to smile. I realised then that I was close to crying and didn't know why.

Tim came to see me once they were back.

'Did you have a good holiday?' I asked.

'No,' he said and did not expand. As he was leaving he said, 'Come over later and talk to Miranda. I want to know if you think she's normal.'

I went an hour later and she opened the door to me. She looked at me and then turned and I followed her. She led the way into the kitchen where Tim was supervising Hayden's evening meal. By now, Miranda's tummy was quite rounded.

'When's the baby due?' I asked, for something to say.

'In four months,' she said. 'A girl.'

'Miranda…' Tim started. She looked at him and then turned to me. 'Tim thinks it's another boy. He says the scan showed that. But what do they know, those people at the hospital? They haven't looked into it as I have. They don't engage with the meaning.'

'Right,' I said. At the time I thought she was talking about the invasiveness of doctors and how they forget that we live with our bodies all the time and know them better than they do. Now, looking back, I see that she meant something else that only she could understand.

I only talked to her once more before the baby was born. It was a few months later at the library early on a Friday evening. This time she was handing back her satchel full of books. I had just taken out two novels to read over the weekend and we left together. We walked side by side, she looked straight ahead and I tried to think of something I could talk to her about.

As we turned the corner into the street where we both lived, she said, without looking at me, 'I have discovered the perfidy of books.'

'Oh?' I wondered what she meant.

'Yes,' she continued. 'For years I have trusted them to help me on my journey. Then, when I was reading yesterday, I realised that the only thing they have to give is words.'

'Right.'

'And words strung together just make sentences. Or rubbish. Depending on the structure. Sentences strung together just make paragraphs, or rubbish. How can you know the difference? Only because of convention. That's all. Custom and use. Nothing profound. Then if you go the other way, all that words are made of is letters. They in themselves are just composed of strokes and curves. Same story. How do you know which set of strokes and curves are a letter, which combination of letters makes a word? Same answer. Because people have decided what is what. That's all. So why bother?'

'I see,' I said. I was scared. Maybe, I thought, Tim was

right, Miranda was quite mad. I considered that as I poured a can of soup into a pan and put it on the gas to heat. I continued thinking about it as I made toasted cheese. I tried to read as I ate my evening meal but my head was full of Miranda and what she had said to me.

When Tim came to see me the next afternoon he said, 'Miranda has decided to spend the rest of her pregnancy in bed.'

'Is she sick?' I asked.

'She is mentally ill.'

'Are you sure?' I asked.

'No.' He shook his head. Then he began to cry, his head in his hands as he let out deep, rusty sobs.

I sat opposite him and waited. I was scared to touch him after the last time I'd tried. I looked down at Hayden who was sitting quietly on the floor looking up at us. I realised then that what I had characterised as his solemn look was in fact a puzzled expression. He was trying to make sense of his world. I resisted an impulse to pick him up and smother him with cuddles.

Finally, Tim reached into his pocket for a tissue. He wiped his eyes and blew his nose. 'It's me. That's what it is. I am inadequate and I have driven her mad.'

'Pregnant women are strange. Their behaviour is driven by hormones. Wait until the baby is born. Then she'll come back to normal,' I said.

'She has not been normal since she's been with me,' Tim said. We sat in silence drinking our tea. I thought about telling Tim that there was a contradiction in his logic. If he'd never known her to be normal, how could he be the cause of her madness? I said nothing.

Over the following weeks Tim's visits were intermittent. The last time I saw him before the baby was born, he said, 'I fell in love with Miranda because she is beautiful and she was quiet and self-contained. I thought she'd be an easy woman to live with.' As we stood in the hall before he left, he put his arms round me and kissed me. We stopped because Hayden had pushed himself between us. The new baby, a boy, was born two days later.

Tim came round the next Saturday. He brought the big pram with the baby at one end and Hayden at the other. When I asked how Miranda was, he said, 'She's convinced that this little one is a daughter, although it's obvious he's not. She calls him Eve.'

Later he said, 'I have to look after her. I married her. So...' He couldn't finish but I knew he was telling me to forget the kiss of the previous week.

Before he left – he stayed only for quarter of an hour and did not drink his tea – he asked, 'Is she really mad? Is she?' I told him I didn't know.

But I did know as I held his son in my arms and watched Miranda walk away. Trying to rid my mind of the image of what I'd just seen – this baby held by his wrist and dangling by his mother's side – I closed my eyes. When I opened them again, she was turning the corner. And then she was gone.

Living in the Wrong Place

It will do, James thought, as the agent unlocked the door and they walked into a small hall. There was a flight of narrow stairs and two open doors, one leading into a living area, the other into a kitchen. There was a smell of new paint but the carpet was stained and the window panes were smudged and grimy.

'It will do,' James said walking into the living room, turning around, wanting to escape the tight uncomfortable feeling that had assailed him most days over the last few months.

'You've not seen it all, yet,' the agent said, jiggling the keys in her hand. 'There's a big bedroom upstairs, a bathroom, separate toilet, and a second smaller room. You could use it as your study.'

'It will do, 'James said. Anywhere would do, as long as there was somewhere to sleep and somewhere to work. He followed the agent up the stairs. 'When can I move in?'

'As soon as you like,' the agent said, shrugging, staring at James as if he was behaving oddly.

His mobile rang as he was driving home. He stopped the car and grabbed the phone. Melissa, he thought, 'Melissa,' he said. But the call was work related. An aggrieved client wondering when James would deliver the brochure he had been contracted to write. It was already a week late.

'Soon,' James said and was told that was not good enough. 'Today would be best, failing that tomorrow at the latest,' the client said, his voice clipped as he went on about what he needed and what James had promised him. James stared out of the car window and listened. When the tirade had finished he said, 'OK,' and ended the call.

That afternoon he arranged for the remaining furniture to be shifted to the place he had rented, he sat at his PC and forced himself to finish the overdue brochure. When it was done, he was exhausted. After Melissa lost the baby when she was five months pregnant, he had felt unbearably sad for a few weeks. He had even cried. He had held Melissa and tried to comfort her. But the sadness had been replaced by a feeling, maybe emptiness or anxiety, which he couldn't name or describe. Nor could he understand why he found it hard to do anything. Work slowed down, even getting dressed in the morning, cleaning his teeth at night became arduous tasks. When Melissa left, he did nothing for nearly a week. When she came to tell him that she would never be back, she also told him to stop feeling sorry for himself. She held herself aloof as she walked around the house deciding what she would take, and what he could have.

'I've contacted an agent to sell it, but you can buy my share if you want to,' she said.

'No,' James said. They were standing by the doorway in the room they had begun to prepare for the baby. He reached for her hand but she pulled it away.

Finally the removal men left and James began the slow job of unpacking and organising his new home. After a while, he made a cup of coffee and took it into the small scrubby garden. He stood leaning against the back wall wishing he could feel normal, wondering if he ever would. Shouting came from the adjacent house and a door banged. James thought he could hear a child crying and he went to look over the low fence that divided his garden from the neighbouring one. A little girl was standing in the middle of the uncut lawn. She had bare feet and was wearing a long T-shirt that was too big for her and came almost to her knees. Her face was thin, dirty and tear-streaked but she was no longer crying; her wavy hair was a dull gold and needed brushing. She stared at James and he was struck by the intensity of her look. There was something knowing, almost adult in the way she held herself.

'Who are you?' she asked, her voice husky.

'I'm James. I live here now,' he said. She continued to stare.

'What's your name?' he asked.

'Maisie and yesterday was my birthday. I turned six. My brothers are Henry and Aaron. '

'I see,' James said. Not sure what else to say, not sure if he should carry on talking or go back inside.

'My mum's cross with me today,' Maisie said. 'She says she has too much to do.'

'Ah,' James said. Maisie was standing still, her arms straight by her side.

A window opened in the next-door house and a woman shouted, 'Inside now, madam, your tea's going cold.'

Maisie shrugged, a grown-up gesture. 'I better go.' She turned and walked away.

That evening James heard more shouting from next door. A few screams, a woman crying, then silence. He sat up in bed, listening, wondering what he should do. Nothing, he decided.

When James went into the garden the following morning, bringing a chair to sit on and a cup of coffee, the woman from next door was pegging out washing. She was thin, dressed in leggings and a skimpy top. When she turned to nod at him he saw that her face was lined and sad. She came to the fence and put both hands on it. Her nails were bitten and the skin around then was raw and flaking.

'I'm Rose,' she said. 'Live here with my man and three kids.'

James introduced himself. 'I met your daughter last evening,' he added.

'You don't want to take notice of her, she's….' Rose stopped. A child had started to cry, making a strange guttural noise. Rose bent down and when she stood up again she was holding a little boy. He was pale, with almost white hair, his head nodded oddly as he wailed and his nose was snotty.

'Better take him inside,' Rose said and left. James peered over the fence. A plastic basket still full of damp clothes was lying on its side on the grass.

That day James managed to work on some of his assignments. Once he'd made a decent living as a freelance technical writer. In the late afternoon he heard children's voices coming from next door and he went into the garden and over to the fence. Maisie was there and an older boy.

'Hello,' James said and Maisie came closer to him. He noticed that the washing had gone.

'Henry's bossing me about. He wants me to play football,' Maisie said. Henry scowled. He had a big bruise on one of his arms.

'Pete did that,' Maisie said, pointing. Henry made a shuddering motion.

'Have you got juice in your house? Can we come and see you?' Maisie asked.

'You'd better ask your mum first,' James said.

'She's asleep.'

'Well,' James said.

'She won't mind,' Maisie said.

'All right,' James said. He went back into the house and let the children in through the front door.

'I have orange juice,' he said and poured each of the children a glass. When he'd finished his, Henry said he was going home.

'What about you, Maisie?' James asked.

'I want to stay. Does anyone else live here with you?'

'No.'

Maisie was staring at him in that same intense way he'd noticed yesterday.

'Are you all right?' James asked.

Maisie frowned. 'Course I am. You're a funny man,' she said.

'Am I?'

She nodded. 'Pete's not my dad. Me and Henry have another dad but we don't see him.'

'Is Pete nice?'

Maisie didn't answer.

'I think it's time for you to go home,' James said. 'I'll come with you.'

Maisie went straight inside, but James knocked on the door.

'Who is it?' a man yelled.

'Your new neighbour. Thought I'd come and introduce myself.'

The man came to the door. He was tubby, with a big shaven head and tattoos on his arms. James gave his name and the man said he was Pete. He scratched his chin.

'You must come over for a beer some time. Not now, fiancée's not too well.'

That evening James ate pasta with a supermarket-made sauce and thought about the people living next door and what the shouting meant and if Pete was hitting Rose or the children. Maisie had said that Pete had made Henry's bruise. He thought about the odd blond toddler and the guttural noise he made. He felt sad thinking about Maisie, and how even though he'd only met her twice he wanted to protect her. He thought about his own daughter, who had come before she was old enough to live, and how through this coming, he had lost not just a baby but his girlfriend as well, the wedding plans dropped.

Later James felt better, the strange unnameable feeling that gripped him had diminished. He wanted to talk to Melissa. He wanted to tell her about Maisie and her family. Saying her name out loud, he wanted to cry; ridiculous, he told himself, for a grown man.

Some evenings there was no sound from next door, other times there was yelling and screaming. In the afternoons James took to going into his garden when the children were home from school. Sometimes Maisie was there, on her own, or with Henry. One morning when Rose was in the garden, hanging out washing, James went out and asked if it was all right for her children to visit him.

'Why would you want them?' Rose asked. James wasn't sure how to answer. Maisie was the one he wanted to see. He'd started buying fruit and biscuits so that he'd have something to offer her if she came over again.

'Well?' Rose said, frowning.

'I could baby-sit one night, so you and Pete could go out.'

Rose snorted. 'You're an odd one.'

'Am I?' James asked.

'How come you're on your own?'

'Ah… it's a long story.' James didn't want to tell it.

'Anyway if you want the kids over, I won't object.' Rose laughed. She turned and went back into her house.

That afternoon Maisie was in the garden on her own.

'Would you like to come to my house?' James asked her. She sat at the kitchen table, ate two chocolate biscuits and drank orange juice.

'Pete doesn't hit me,' she said, watching as James cut a pear into quarters for her.

'That's good.' James passed her the plate of pear. She picked up a piece and looked at it, frowning. She bit into it, suspicious. When she'd eaten all the fruit, her chin was sticky. James passed her some kitchen paper and said she should use it to clean her face. She stared at him and then did as he suggested. There was something flirty in the way she sat opposite him, one thin shoulder raised higher than the other.

'I think it's time for you to go home,' James said.

'Don't want to. I want to watch your TV. Mum always puts baby things on for Aaron. He's nearly three but he can't talk. He's actually dumb. That's what Mum says. She says it and then she cries. Actually he can't walk properly either.'

James turned on the TV and flicked through the channels until he found something he thought she'd like. He watched her watching the television and wished he could ask her if she was being treated properly. What Pete did to her, if anything, what he did to Rose, to Henry. He would like to have picked up the little girl, sit her on his knee and hold her. That wouldn't do, wouldn't do at all.

The house he'd shared with Melissa was sold, the mortgage paid, his share of the money in his account. The last tie. Probably he would never see her again, never talk to her. Then she telephoned.

'Just to say goodbye,' she said.

'I know,' James said.

'And to find out if you're doing OK.'

'I'm managing to work more.'

'That's good. Are you seeing friends?'

'Our friends were mainly your friends.'

'Not all of them, James. There's Bob and Trev. You should call them. Meet for a beer or something.'

'All right. I will.' He might, James thought, he might call. Perhaps ask them both over for a Sunday lunch barbecue. Maybe.

'So…' Melissa was getting ready to finish the call.

'The thing is… I need to talk to you,' James said.

'No, James, no.'

'I need your advice.'

Melissa sighed. 'Go ahead.'

So he told her about the family next door, about Pete and possible violence, about the little boy who couldn't talk or walk properly, about Henry's bruises, about Maisie and her vulnerability and also her strange knowingness, as if she was already aware of what her life would be about.

'Don't get involved. Don't. Find somewhere else to live. They're not your problem.'

'I feel such tenderness towards her. As if…'

'She's not yours, James. She can't replace…'

'No.'

When the call was over James phoned Bob, then Trev, arranged to meet them at a bar in town the following Saturday.

James was woken by his doorbell ringing late on Sunday morning. He'd drunk too much the night before. The bell rang again. He sat up in bed and rubbed his head. He pulled on jeans and a T-shirt and went to open the door. There was Maisie. She walked past him and into the kitchen. She sat at the table.

'Juice?' James asked. He poured a glass for each of them. He opened the biscuit tin and put it on the table.

'Apple?' he asked. Maisie shook her head.

'Why do grown-ups stay in bed in the mornings?' she asked.

'I don't normally. I came home very late last night.'

'Can I watch your TV?'

'All right,' James said. When she was settled in front of it, he went upstairs, showered, dressed in clean clothes, came down, drank a glass of water and took two Panadol.

He went into the living room, sat down, leant back and closed his eyes.

'You've gone to sleep again.' Maisie was standing in front of him. She had turned the TV off.

'Sorry,' James said. He looked at his watch. 'Isn't it your lunchtime? Perhaps you should go home.'

'I don't think so,' Maisie said. 'Henry's got a cut on his leg where Pete hit him with a knife. Pete's always angry.'

'He doesn't hit you, though, does he?'

'No. He says girls are too soft to hit. He doesn't hit Mum, either, he just squeezes her to make her shut up. He doesn't hit Aaron, neither. He wants him to go into a home.'

'What sort of home?'

Maisie didn't answer. 'You can take me to McDonalds. I went there for my birthday. I had chips.'

'All right. Perhaps we'd better invite Henry too. We'll go and ask your mum.'

When Rose answered the door, she was wearing a shabby dressing gown and looked exhausted and as if she'd been crying.

'Yes, you can take Maisie, but not Henry. He's not well,' she said.

The following Saturday when the doorbell rang Pete was there, holding a six pack.

'Fancy a beer?' he said and James led him into the living room and switched off the TV. Pete passed him a can, took one for himself and sat down, leaning back, legs apart, already drunk.

'Just thought we should get to know each other.' Pete burped. 'You're not married?'

'No.'

'Me neither. Rose and me started to live together when she fell for Aaron.'

'Right,' James said.

The first cans were finished and Pete handed out a second round. He talked about women he'd known, how difficult it was raising other people's kids.

'That Maisie, she's a hard case. You don't want to believe the half of what she tells you. Makes things up,' Pete said as he reached for a third can.

When Pete had finished his fourth beer, James apologised, saying he'd no more booze. He'd bring something round next weekend to make up for it.

'We could go to the pub,' Pete said.

'Another time,' James said. He sat and waited for Pete to go. Instead he fell asleep, lying back in the chair, snoring.

He would have to shift, James decided. Monday he'd start looking for a new place. He thought about Maisie and how he was deserting her. But Melissa was right, she wasn't his child, she wasn't his problem.

In the evenings the shouting became worse. Several nights in a row. When James went into the garden in the late afternoons, it was empty. On Friday he took his morning coffee and sat on his chair, holding his face to the sun. Another two weeks and he'd be gone from this place. He'd found a new unit to rent in the centre of town and a young couple were to take over this tenancy. Maybe they'd befriend Maisie, look after her a bit.

'Hey James.' He opened his eyes. Rose was standing at the fence, staring at him in a manner reminiscent of her daughter.

'Rose.' He stood up.

'He's gone. Pete's gone.' Rose sounded angry and as if James was responsible for him leaving.

'I'm sorry.'

Rose snorted, turned and stomped back into her house.

That afternoon Maisie was in the garden. She came up to the fence as he went out.

'I'm not allowed to talk to you anymore,' she whispered. Her thin face was tear-streaked, her eyes huge. She stood still and stared at him. 'Mum says you can't be my friend.'

'But I am your friend,' James said.

Maisie nodded as if she knew far more than a six-year-old should know.

The police came the next day, two of them.

'I did nothing to her, nothing,' he said when they explained why they were there. The man shook his head, the woman looked away and sighed.

Deadheading the Roses

Three years ago, Dylan, who lives next door, slid off the roof. The fall didn't kill him but now he is unable to walk or talk. He communicates by blinking. One for no, two for yes, several when the right questions aren't being asked.

I think about that day as I chop onions and stare out of my kitchen window at the roof in question. It was a hot Sunday and I was in the garden tending to tomatoes and having an imaginary argument with Jack, my husband, about his laziness in general and the unmown lawn in particular. I looked up and saw Dylan perched up high, one arm around the chimney stack, but thought nothing of it. He was twenty, had decided that he would drop out of university and was into experimenting. I waved at him but he didn't wave back. Didn't even see me. I'd spoken to him not long before and he'd told me that he was searching for a way of making sense of life.

'I know that humans need to name things to make them real. I'm trying to imagine things without names. But that may be impossible,' he said. His mother, Josie, who has been my best friend since we moved here when Jack and I were just married and believed that sexual love was real, wondered whether Dylan was taking drugs.

'He's always been like that,' I said. I first met him when he was two. Josie and I used to sit and drink coffee together and he would stand with his hands on my knee and stare at me. He could keep that up for several minutes, then he'd sigh in an adult way and turn away. Later, when he'd become alarmingly articulate for a small boy, he told me he was trying to work out what made people different from each other and as Josie and I looked alike (both round-faced with blonde hair and blue eyes) he was comparing my features with those of his mother. The day before the roof incident, I'd told her not to worry about Dylan.

'Not drugs. He's probably some sort of genius,' I suggested. A little grudgingly as none of my three children were showing signs of being anything but normal.

'Well,' Josie said. Both pleased and not pleased. Her husband, Tom, had recently left her. Said that now Sammie, their youngest kid, had only one year left at school he could do what he always wanted. He'd taken only those things he could carry on his motorbike and had ridden away. Lauren, Josie's first daughter, a year older than Dylan, had been planning to go and live with her boyfriend; instead she moved him into her mother's house saying that it would be good to have a man about the place.

'What about me?' Dylan asked her.

'I said "a man",' Lauren retorted and Dylan shrugged and smiled, not caring. He really didn't mind what others thought of him. Josie and I were on her terrace sharing a bottle of wine at the time, trying to decide if Josie should celebrate her freedom or mourn the loss of her husband. I was for the former but Josie was wavering between the two.

'How would you feel if Jack left you?' she asked.

'Wonderful,' I said. I meant it. Like Dylan, I, too, was trying to make sense of life. How could all that lust and hope and planning lead to boredom and sameness? When did that young man who made my head and heart spin turn into an old codger with a soft tummy and sagging buttocks who enjoyed farting in bed and grunted in annoyance when I put an arm over him? Every day was more or less the same. Wake to the alarm, make sure the kids ate breakfast before leaving for school, remind Jack about his packed lunch in the fridge, off to work, back home, cook dinner and do household chores. A bit of boring telly and into bed.

'I'll be the one to leave. When Beth finishes school.' Like Josie I had three children: girl, boy, girl. Lily was then seventeen, Gareth fifteen and Beth thirteen. Hers were Lauren, then Dylan; Sammie, her younger girl was the same age as Lily. Lauren frowned at me and told me not to be silly, of course I wouldn't go, women like me didn't do that sort of thing. She sniffed, sure of herself, sure of us all. Dylan stepped off the terrace and cartwheeled the length of the lawn, ending up in the rose-bed.

'Ah,' I say as I finish chopping the onions. I'd looked up from my gardening that hot Sunday, disturbed by a rasping sound coming from Josie's roof and I saw Dylan sliding down the tiles. I heard a squashy bang and for a moment I stood, mouth open, before rushing next door. Whenever I think of that moment, I can smell the pungent scent of tomato. I can no longer eat pizza or spaghetti bolognaise.

Tom came back briefly when Dylan was first in hospital but went away again soon after. I think it was because he felt that there was nothing he could do to make Dylan right again. He would have preferred his son to have died and then we could mourn, and have a funeral and talk about him with tears of loss. He couldn't cope with sitting by a broken body with no voice.

Josie insisted that he came home. I helped her. We made sure that she got everything she was entitled to. Stuff to make it easier to move him, an hour or so of daily nursing help, respite care from time to time, grants and allowances now that she had given up working and become Dylan's carer. Because she was his mother, the financial aid was minimal.

'It would cost the state a heap more to keep him in hospital,' we told the social workers, the bureaucrats who gave the forms that had to be filled in. I wondered how those working close to the ill and the disabled could be so hard.

'Probably they'll let him die – help him die – if we leave him there,' Josie said one bitter evening as we shared a bottle of wine after a gruelling day preparing for Dylan's homecoming. What she didn't say, but I knew she was thinking, was that some time he might be able to speak again. Especially because he'd told us he was going to be a writer. Even when he was little he loved to talk; loved to use words and phrases that surprised. I think now of all the sentences filling his head that he has decided not to share with us. I wish we could put a siphon in and draw them out. When he was still in hospital we searched his room for diaries, jottings, we went through his PC looking for the novel he'd said he was planning. But there was nothing. Not a thing.

'He would have written. Quite soon. He was getting ready for it. Just…' Time ran out for him. Josie couldn't say that last phrase, instead tears spilled out of her eyes over her cheeks, under her chin and down her neck wetting the collar of her blouse.

She doesn't get used to it. She's learned to cope. That's what she tells me. Every morning she wakes up and knows something bad has happened and then she remembers. She cries for a few minutes, getting it done for the day.

I need to talk to her. I look at the pile of chopped onions and feel nauseous. I gag a few times and then wash my hands at the kitchen sink. Jack and Beth will have to get their own meal this evening, I can't bear to cook. I call out as I leave, telling them where I'm going. Beth is in her room pretending to be doing her homework but either listening to music or talking to a friend on her phone. She won't have heard me. Jack is playing a computer game and although my words penetrate his brain, they don't morph into meaning; nothing I say to him has done for a long time.

I ring the bell and walk into Josie's house. She's sitting in the room where Dylan lives, the remains of his meal on the table beside him. His eyes are closed.

'Good,' she says when she sees me. 'I'll open some wine.'

'Not on my account,' I say and she frowns. We go into

the kitchen and she takes a bottle from the fridge. I follow her onto the terrace and we sit in our usual chairs. She pours the wine. Two glasses in spite of what I've said.

A month ago, I told her about The Dude. She laughed.

'Are you going to leave Jack for him?' she'd asked.

'I wouldn't leave Jack for a man with no name,' I said. 'Although I will be going.' All the time that Dylan had been lying paralysed and speechless, I had been waiting for a time when my life would change. I imagined walking out of my house with a small suitcase and never coming back. The idea made me feel good... no, more than that, euphoric. There was no plan beyond shutting the door behind me and leaning on it, sighing with satisfaction. Sometimes I indulged in an image of boarding a plane or staring through the window of a train at unfamiliar countryside, but nothing more.

'He has a name,' Josie said.

'But I don't use it.'

'Perhaps I can share The Dude then, it's been so long.'

'Of course,' I said. I thought of bringing him around to Josie's house. Ringing her bell and going, leaving him on the doorstep for her to welcome in.

'So,' she says now. 'How's The Dude?'

'Gone,' I say. She puts her head on one side, and pulls a face. In spite of her joke about sharing The Dude, she finds it hard to understand that I only wanted him for a quick fling. A way of remembering how sex could be. 'But,' I say.

'Oh no,' she says. She's understood.

'Yes,' I say. 'I haven't decided yet. Keep it or... abort it.'

'What will Jack say if you have to tell him?'

'Oh. I'll say it's his.'

'And… is that possible?'

I nod.

'How do sensible women in their early forties get accidentally pregnant? I assume it is an accident. ' Josie's mouth is sceptically pursed.

I shrug. 'Carelessness. Been on the pill for years. Came off it and forgot the consequences… '

'So it is The Dude's.'

I shrug again. 'Could be Jack's,' I say, eyeing Josie's glass of cool white wine as she raises it to her lips.

'You can have some if you're going to get rid of it,' she says, pointing at the second glass, frowning at my tummy.

I shake my head. It's not just – I won't call it a baby, if I did then abortion would become almost impossible – to protect the foetus, it's because I know that alcohol would make me feel sick. Already I am aware of incipient nausea. And I don't like it. I don't want to be pregnant. I want to be free; I want to imagine myself leaving home in two years when Beth is eighteen. The decision should be easy; already I should have contacted my doctor, set the process in motion. I'm hesitating but I feel that I would be killing a person. I don't want to think that. I try not to.

'So you might keep it,' Josie says and after I explain my ambivalence, she continues, 'Don't be silly. It's nothing yet. If you don't want it, let it go. That's how to think of it.'

'Would you?' I ask.

'Of course,' she says and pours more wine in her glass.

'Well,' I say and look away. She knows what I'm thinking. We have discussed it on and off since she came to accept that Dylan would neither walk nor talk again.

The first time she suggested that it might be best for him to be helped to die, and that maybe one day she'd find the courage to do just that, I didn't say anything for a while although I agreed with her. But that's easy for me. I'm not his mother.

Then I asked, 'Would you be doing it for him or for you?'

'If I thought that it was in any way for me I couldn't do it,' she said. I had offended her, I could see. She wiped away tears with the back of her hand and I felt most dreadfully guilty at even considering that her motive might be selfish.

'Sorry,' I said.

Her sobs became louder. 'There is an element of… not wanting this to be all I do for the rest of my life.' She bent her head, sucking in air to fuel her desperate grief.

Now she says, 'It's not the same. Dylan is my son. You just have… an inconvenience in your womb.'

I sigh and watch as she takes a sip from her glass. I imagine having the baby and giving him to Josie as replacement for Dylan. It would have to be a boy. Her two girls are troublesome; Lauren, who is now married, always knows better than her mother how things should be done and Sammie is wild, promiscuous and running up debt. Lauren of course, knows exactly how Josie should treat her younger daughter. She also thinks that Dylan should be put in a home.

'Would you like another child?' I ask and Josie frowns at me.

'I could never replace Dylan,' she says, her voice harsh.

'No,' I agree.

'Do you want me to help? With organising the... procedure.' She nods at my tummy.

'I suppose... yes,' I say. 'And...'

'I could never help Dylan to die. I've come to realise that,' she says.

'But?'

She opens her mouth in a sort of tight yawn. It's her way of stopping the tears from coming. 'Yes... and... he'd like to see you soon.'

I leave soon after that. Tomorrow I will make an appointment with my doctor. Josie is coming with me, she insists, she will arrange for a carer to sit with Dylan for an hour or so.

I've come to talk to Dylan. This is not unusual as I visit him often. I sit with him when Josie has to shop or just needs a few hours away from the house. I tell him lots, but nothing he shouldn't know. I haven't mentioned The Dude or the pregnancy. I haven't said that I was thinking of running away once Beth leaves school in two years' time. That would be mean, moaning about how I wanted to be free from my marriage, my life, the relentless sameness of it all, when all he's able to do is listen. And blink. He looks at me intently not because he likes to hear what I'm saying but because it's his only expression now. When he was a little boy, he often had a puzzled look: a little frown with the insides of his eyebrows pointing up like question marks. Josie used to bring him over when I was pregnant with my first child and she with her third. He liked to pat our huge tummies and ask over and over what the babies were doing inside, how did they get there, how and when would they get out. Sometimes Josie would leave him with me while she went to fetch Lauren from pre-school. He would press his face against my bulge and tell the baby what life was like on the outside.

As I open the door into his room, I'm thinking about how sweet he was and how I loved him before my children came. Once Lily was born, he stopped being my favourite child. Of course. But now that he's trapped in his useless body, I feel guilty that I let him go so easily. I sometimes imagine a scene in which I was able to prevent what happened. In hospital after the accident doctors asked if he had meant to fall. 'No,' Beth said. 'No, no, no.' Sometimes I wondered. Still wonder. It's not a question I've been able to ask him, though. I screw my eyes closed and see him on the roof, holding on to the chimney. I could have kept him safe if I'd not stopped looking at him. I could have held him with my gaze. Silly, I tell myself. But.

I sit on the chair so that I can look at his face. His eyes are open. He would smile at me if he could. Or so I like to think.

'Your mum says you have something important you want to talk to me about,' I say. He blinks once. I pick up the signing board we've made, covered with a few words and groups of letters that we use to communicate. 'Do you want to ask me something?' Again one blink. I pause, not knowing where to go next. He blinks several times and makes the strange strangled noise that is his only sound. 'Sorry,' I say. 'Shall we use the board?' One blink. I point to the word 'vowel'. Two blinks: no. We've worked out a system. Vowels we do one by one but consonants are sorted into seven sets of three. We tried, Josie and I, once he'd settled at home – if 'settle' is the right word – to encourage him to write. He could tell us what he wanted to say and we would record it for him.

'You could begin on your novel,' Josie said to him.

'Or maybe some short stories,' I suggested. Two blinks for both of us and then his eyes closed. We've mentioned it several times but he's never wanted to. 'Too much in my head to let out through nods,' he told us eventually through the board. Indeed, he finds it tiring just to tell his mum what he would like to eat or the music he wants to listen to on his iPod. Sometimes he can't be bothered to communicate or he makes up nonsense words.

Now he wants to tell me what is troubling him and although it's tedious, I have finally figured out what he needs to say and I turn to look out of the window. I feel, too, as if I'm not in this room with him but a long way away in a place where sounds are muted and colours pale. What he said was, with a directness that is often lacking in his communication, 'I want to die now. I can't ask Mum so will you do it for me?'

'Dylan,' I say eventually, my face still turned from him. 'Why now?' I think of the months and months he's lain here often on his own. He has a radio and a TV as well as an iPod, but often all he wants is to gaze out of the window that I'm now staring through. I force myself to look at him, he blinks several times, and there's a clenching feeling in my womb.

I raise the board and start again to collect what he wants to say. Once it's made I let the sentences settle in my brain. 'There's nothing more in my head. My words have dissolved,' he has told me. I let my tears fall. I tell him that I love him. I start to say that what he's asking me to do is very hard. But I stop myself. Far less hard for me to put a cushion over his face and hold it there till he dies than for him to lie motionless day after day after day. It would not be murder, I tell myself. I would do it because I cared for him. And for Josie.

'I love you,' I say again. 'And I need to think about this. Is that OK?' He blinks once and we stare at each other. I lean over and stroke his cheek, his chin. I touch his lips with my finger. He blinks and blinks and makes his only sound. Before I leave him, I give him a drink of water and then I'm in the hallway, leaning against the wall. I am exhausted. My legs are trembling. I don't want to have to think or plan or make decisions. I realise that I haven't asked Dylan if I can discuss what he's asked me to do with his mother. When I return to his room he's asleep.

The doctor is not sympathetic when I tell him that I would like a termination. He gives me a lecture on the right of a child to be born. I sit with gritted teeth and think of Josie in the waiting room, reading silly magazines. I think of what she would say if I tell her that I've been persuaded to continue with the pregnancy. The doctor drones on using a sorrowful voice.

'I wouldn't have expected this of you,' he says. I stare at him, trying to close my ears. He has been our doctor since I became pregnant with Lily, but I didn't realise that he was anti abortion. Mostly I've been to the surgery with the children: minor ailments, vaccinations, yearly check-ups. 'Many women regret it later. I know of several who are still mourning after several years have passed.'

'I'm forty-two. My family is complete.'

'Not a blessing then?' he asks with a silly smile and I make my mind up. 'No,' I say, standing up. I ask him to refer me to the specialist and tell him if he won't, I'll find a doctor who will. He sighs and does what I want.

Josie goes to the counter to buy the coffee and I sit, waiting, feeling as if my life is not mine, has never been mine. I think of my children; Lily away at university already engaged, Gareth just left school with no idea of what he wants to do next, Beth, self-absorbed, hardly noticing me except as a provider of food, clean clothes and pocket money. Maybe the one in my womb would turn out different. I mean different in the sense of unusual, like Dylan. If I put a cushion over his face and held it there until he stopped breathing, would I consider myself a killer? None of this is real, not thinking about my actual children nor the one that… won't be, nor about helping Dylan to die. Josie arrives with the coffee. She is smiling. She is enjoying being out of the house and indulging in a visit to the café. I try to smile back but now I am thinking of her son's request and what I should say to Josie.

'I spoke to Dylan,' I say. I look at her as I sip from my cup. She nods.

'Do you want… to… ask me anything?'

Her smile has gone and she looks away and then back at me. 'Do what he asks you, if you can. But… don't tell me about it.'

'Won't you want to know… before?'

She shakes her head. There are tears in her eyes. I have spoiled the outing. Not I exactly, because Dylan is always there – will always be there – but I have reminded her that her life is broken.

I tell Dylan that I will do it. I ask him if he's sure that's what he wants. He blinks once. I tell him that the idea makes me sad and that he will have to wait as I have something else to do first.

'Is that OK?' I ask. He blinks. Just the once.

I have told myself I would not be a murderer. That what I was planning to do was an act of mercy, of love. I thought about being caught and charged with causing the death. This would not happen. I don't know why but I knew that unless I told, no one would suspect that I had held a pillow over Dylan's face and waited for him to leave the body that he no longer wanted to occupy. I thought, often and often, every hour of the day and waking at dawn, about releasing Dylan. I went through the motions in my mind; I practised how I would feel. I was getting ready to do what I could for Dylan. And I knew it was what Josie wanted. Sometimes the idea scared me but the act was becoming increasingly certain.

As for my own predicament, I have been wavering, discussing the abortion with Josie.

'I'm just being selfish,' I have said. 'Why should I deny this child a life?'

'Don't be silly. You don't want it and it's not a child yet.'

I didn't reply, as I couldn't say that because of Dylan and what he had asked me to do, I wasn't sure that I was strong enough to deny life to a healthy foetus.

'And,' Josie continued, 'what life would it have if it got born? A slob for a father, a mother that resented it. What's more, I've been looking at the statistics and you could well miscarry.'

'But…'

'I'll come with you, when you have it done,' Josie said firmly. She raised her chin, tightened her mouth and glared at me.

'I'll… think about it,' I said.

The day before the abortion is scheduled, I wake in the early hours and feel the night heavy all about. I get up and go downstairs and out into the garden. I sit on the bench and look up at the moon, pale in the dark sky and I know that if I decide to keep the foetus, I will not be able to help Dylan.

Josie is in the garden; she is deadheading her roses. I saw her from my kitchen and now I am in Dylan's room and she doesn't know I'm here.

'Is it time?' I ask him. He blinks. 'Sure?' He blinks again. I lean to kiss him and he's blinking over and over. 'The board?' I ask.

He spells out that that he loves me and understands what we are both doing. It's taking time and I'm getting nervous that Josie will come in and find me here. It's essential she doesn't know when it's to be done. Dylan has spelled this out. Josie has said – hinted – that it's what she wants. I kiss Dylan again, raise the pillow and press it on his face. I am crying. I am mourning this lovely lost boy and the other one who barely lived for a short time inside me. I feel Dylan leaving. I do. The room is filled with heaviness and then empties.

As soon as I move the pillow away, I am overwhelmed with sadness and with the enormity of what I've done. I start to gulp in air and feel the tears welling up from deep inside. I look at Dylan's face. I was hoping to see it peaceful and at rest. But it's not. It is etched with his suffering and I run out of his room, of Josie's house, remembering to close the doors carefully so as not to make a noise. In my bedroom, my sobs explode.

I need to compose myself for when Josie finds Dylan. I want to shout and throw things about the room. I go into the bathroom, turn on all the taps and scream. Then I vomit, leaning over the toilet bowl until it feels as if everything inside me has been rejected.

I have calmed myself, washed my face, brushed my hair, applied a little make-up by the time I hear Josie calling, her voice sharpened with grief. I open the window, lean through it and see her standing in the gap between our houses. She is still holding the secateurs and a dead rose has attached itself to her skirt.

Later that night we sit on her terrace long after dark, crying from time to time and talking about Dylan, our other children, the shape of our lives and how we will cope with the future.

After the funeral, we gather at Josie's house. I stay after everyone else has left. Even Lauren and her husband have gone, taking Tom, Dylan's father, with them. The day is nearly over. I help Josie clear away and, as usual, we sit on the terrace but with cups of tea instead of wine.

'Finally, when you did it, was it hard?' she asks. I look at her and wonder that she should be asking as we had silently agreed never to talk about it.

'The abortion,' she explains.

'Yes,' I say. 'But it's for the best.' Those are the words to be used, both for my baby and for Dylan. I don't yet know if I mean them. What I am sure of is that I will never feel free again.

Background and acknowledgements for the stories

- 'Dead is Dead' was published in *takahé* 62 in 2007, in 2004 broadcast on Radio New Zealand and in 2003 short-listed in the South Island Writers' Association (SIWA) Short Story Competition, open to residents of New Zealand

- 'My Beautiful Dad' was long-listed in the 2010 Fish Publishing Annual International Short Story Competition

- 'Matilda the Determined Woman' was long listed in the 2012 Fish Publishing Annual International Short Story Competition

- 'One of Those Days' was published in the *International Literary Quarterly* and was long-listed in the 2008 Fish Publishing Annual International Short Story Competition

- 'Runners' was included in 'Crest to Crest', an anthology of pieces featuring the district of Canterbury, New Zealand, published in 2009

- 'Polly's Day' was broadcast on Radio New Zealand in 2010

- 'My Father Talked to my Silent Mother' was broadcast on Radio New Zealand in 2009 and in 2008 was short-listed in the Western Districts Short Story Competition, open to residents of New Zealand

- 'The Love Story of a Feckless Man' was published in *Bravado* 16 in 2009, in 2007 was short-listed in the SIWA Short Story Competition, open to residents of New Zealand, in 2006 given second place in the Scribendi International Short Story Competition and in 2005 long-listed in the Fish Publishing Annual International Short Story Competition

- 'Escaping the Warm-blooded' was published in JAAM 25 in 2008

- 'Remembering Peter' was broadcast on Radio New Zealand in 2007 and the same year was short-listed in the SIWA Short Story Competition, open to residents of New Zealand

- 'The Homecoming' was a finalist in a Glimmer Train International Short Story Competition in 2006 and in 2007 was broadcast on Radio New Zealand

- 'Cheryl and Me' was published in *takahē* 59 in 2006 and in the same year was highly commended in the Western Districts Short Story Competition, open to residents of New Zealand and published in their anthology. In 2003 it was highly commended in the SIWA Short Story Competition, open to residents of New Zealand and was long-listed in the 2002 Fish Publishing Annual International Short Story Competition

- 'Sweet Susie' was published in *takahē* 61 in 2006

- 'Playing with Clay' was long-listed in the 2005 Fish Publishing Annual International Short Story Competition

- 'The Sleeping Handsome' was included in 'A La Carte', a collection of stories published in 2004, was placed in the 2002 Scribendi International Short Story Competition and published in their anthology

- 'My Name is Erica' was short-listed in the 2002 Writers' Spot International Short Story Competition

- 'Meeting Dad' was broadcast on Radio New Zealand in 2012

- 'This is not Miranda's Story' was short-listed in the 2010 Fish Publishing Annual International Short Story Competition and gained a special mention in the Premier Category (for published writers) of the 2009 Katherine Mansfield New Zealand Wide Short Story Competition

- 'Living in the Wrong Place' was published in *takahē* 85 in 2015

- 'Deadheading the Roses' was short-listed in the 2011 Fish Publishing Annual International Short Story Competition

19424715R00128

Printed in Great Britain
by Amazon